GRACE AND A THUG

GRACE AND A THUG

Book 3
A novel

When God Wants You, There is no Place to Run. and no Place to Hide

Dr. Akeam A. Simmons

iUniverse, Inc.
Bloomington

GRACE And A THUG
When God Wants You, There is no Place to Run, and no Place to Hide

iUniverse books may be ordered through booksellers or by contacting:

iUniverse
1663 Liberty Drive
Bloomington, IN 47403
www.iuniverse.com
1-800-Authors (1-800-288-4677)

ISBN: 978-1-4759-6943-6 (sc)
ISBN: 978-1-4759-6944-3 (ebk)

Library of Congress Control Number: 2012924191

Printed in the United States of America

iUniverse rev. date: 12/21/2012

TO JEHOVAH
The only true and everlasting God

TO THE LADY IN MY DREAMS
THAT FILLS ME WITH PEACE AND WONDER
THAT I CANNOT BUT HOPE FOR THE NEXT TIME
I CLOSE MY EYES

CHAPTER ONE

Snow eased quietly onto the curve just blocks away from Bobo's club. He was driving an old 1965 Chevrolet impala. He had just bought it a few days ago from some youngster in a hood across town. It was his policy to change the cars that he did his dirt in ever so often. He sat there in his black leather suit with a black turtle neck on, and quietly waited with the engine softly purring. DMX sang hard from the CD player about getting even with somebody that had betrayed him.

The music from Bobo's club thumped in every direction, and the smell of smoke mixed with alcohol filled the air. He watched as folks went in and out of Bobo's, still no sign of Whatley; the big black dude that friend and foe called killer. Word was that Whatley earned his name because he had killed so many men, and hadn't done not one day in prison for any of them-though he had been in prison many a times for other crimes for which he boasted upon.

A passing prostitute noticed Snow sitting alone in the car, and eased up, leaned into the window on the passenger side of the car and sweetly and softly said, "Hey sweetie, want to have some fun for a minute?"

Snow didn't say anything. He just stared sternly at her with his deep blue grimacing eyes that were now filled with hate and revenge.

She could not recognize who he was. She just saw the shadowy outline in the dark. "What's wrong? Cat got your tongue? Let me help you forget about your problems." She reached in and softly rubbed Snow's hand.

He reached up on the dash board and grabbed his cigarette lighter. He knew her. She was one of Candy's girlfriends before she was beat to death by Deacon and his boys; so, out of respect for Candy, he endured her for a moment. He remembered that Candy said that Princess was good people that had had some tough breaks.

"Come on, don't be shy. Your business is safe with Princess-that's what everybody calls me around here sugar. Can I get in?"

She started to fumble with the handle of the car while giggling softly. Just then, Snow flicked the cigarette lighter to give a glimpse to her of who she was talking to. Instantly, through the shadows, she peered into blue eyes that were so filled with hate that they looked right through her.

Her knees got weak, and sweat filled her palms as she recognized the white boy with blue eyes and long dreads. "Damn, oh my god, Snow . . . . It's . . . . It's . . . . It's you. They said that you were dead; that you had gotten blown up a few months ago in the house with Doctor Peewee and some of your relative."

"Is that what they say Princess?" He moaned softly without hardly parting his lips.

"Ooh . . . . Ooh, um so glad that you are alive. I felt like all the good people were leaving me-Candy, then you." She quickly got into the car. "They say that Killer and his boys were hired to snuff you out. Your family was just in the wrong place at the wrong time."

"Who hired Killer?"

"Ah . . . . Uh . . . . They say that June bug's daddy hired them." She paused for a moment; waiting for Snow's response-there was none. "I don't know how true it is, but his ass has been flaunting around town last week like he the new man on the block."

"Is that so," said Snow, now very interested in Princess every word.

"He wanted to give me some business the other night, but I told him that I was sick. I ain't fixing to sleep with the devil." She paused, and lowered her head. "I think they all should go to hell; cause all of them had something to do with my girls death . . . . all of them!! If I weren't a woman, I'd kill every one of them for my girl."

"Don't worry, um sending all of them to hell before it is over with," said Snow now holding Princess hand encouragingly. "Now, do me two favors; go into Bobo's and make sure that

Killer and his boys are in there, and where they at; and, if you got any friends in there, you'd better secretly tell them to leave cause all hell is going to break out in just a short time.

"Ok snow . . . . Damn, um so glad you're alive. Can we get together later for some coffee or something?" She said as she exited the car.

Snow knew that Princess had always had a little crush on him, but she kept it at bay because she loved and respected her best friend Candy. He also knew that, like Candy, he could trust Princess. "Yea, sure, give me a call later." He wrote his number down on a piece of paper and handed it to her.

Princess got out of the car and briskly walked down the street to Bobo's club and disappeared in the door amidst the smoke and loud music.

Snow waited patiently as fifteen minutes passed. He grabbed his submachine gun and patted it softly as though it was alive. "We fixing to send a whole lot of folks to hell tonight."

Just then, Princess came out of Bobo's with seven of her girlfriends following her. They stopped a short distance from the front door of the club. Princess said something to the girls, then they turned and walked in the other direction giggling as they went.

Hurriedly she walked to Snow's car; got in and eased the door shut. "Yea, they in there sweetie. They're in the far corner on the left side-all of them. They having a good time celebrating you being gone; so, them niggars in for a big surprise when they see your ass come back from the dead."

Quickly, she leaned into Snow and kissed him softly on the lips. "You know that I've always been into you; I just never acted cause of my girl Candy, and after she was gone, I tried to give you some time to greave." She paused for a moment, and rubbed her hand softly across his brow. "Um still into you Snow, so please come back out of there safely. Don't make me die twice." She turned to get out of the car.

"Wait." Snow reached into a black case in the back seat. "Here, take you some time off until we get together." He handed her a wrapped stack of one hundred dollar bills-10,000.00. She tucked it in her purse.

She started to cry.

"What's wrong?" Snow asked.

"I don't want nothing to happen to you . . . . I don't Snow . . . . I know you got to do what you got to do, but I'll be waiting for your call."

"No, better still," said Snow as he scribbled on a piece of paper in the darkness. "Here is my address on the south side-the only other person knew about my place on the south side was Candy. Now, go there and wait for me." He paused for a moment, then said, "Go buy you some decent clothes. Don't dress like a hooker no more."

"Ok, um a go change then I'll go wait for you." She looked for a moment at the piece of paper with Snow's address on it, then tore it up into tiny little pieces.

"What?" Snow said.

"I'll remember it. Don't want nobody finding your address accidentally."

"That's what um talking about-You're just like Candy was."

"Yea, that was my girl . . . . She would want me to take care of you."

Princess hugged Snow once again, softly kissed him, and then got out of the car. She blew him a kiss and disappeared into the shadows-headed straight for Snow's Southside crib.

He waited in the car for another hour-wanting Killer and his crew to get good and juiced up before he entered. He got out of the car; eased his door shut, and strolled slowly towards Bobo's club. With a baseball cap pulled down over his brow, and his dreads tucked under, he entered Bobo's with the submachine gun hanging to his side up under his coat. Briskly, he walked to the back of the club, and just like Princess had said, there they were huddled up laughing and talking. He stood a few feet from them and glared at them menacingly.

"What's up home boy?" Killer yelled out towards Snow-not knowing it was Snow.

Snow didn't reply; didn't move, he just stared at them. The girls snickered.

"Go see what's up with this clown." Killer said to one of his boys.

Before the man could get up to follow Killer's request, Snow flung his baseball cap to the floor. His golden blond dreads dropped and danced upon his shoulders as he flung his coat back and slowly raised the submachine gun.

"But you're dead." Killer screamed out while reaching for his gun and pulling one of the women in front of him. "What? I got to kill you again?"

"No . . . . No . . . . No . . . . Please Snow," said the woman that Killer had pulled in front of him. "Let me go you freakin coward. Snow please."

"Ham mercy!" Another of Killer's men screamed out as he tried to run away.

Snow squeezed the trigger; the submachine gun started to speak, spitting several bullets at every word. Bullets riddled through Killer and his girl like Swiss cheese before he could even get his gun from his side. He sprayed all of them, and within moments it was over. Killer, the girls, and his boys lay there dying.

Snow felt a little bad for the girls to have to die with Killer and his crew, but it is the chance you risk and the price you pay for choosing to hang out with bad company-like spending too much time with a bunch of snakes; pretty soon you know that you're going to get bit.

"But you dead!" Killer screamed amidst pain. "You dead Snow . . . . You dead."

"Yeaaa," Snow hissed softly. "Um the ghost of judgment."

Snow slowly walked up to him while everybody in the club was running, screaming, hiding and hoping that none of Snow's bullets had their names on them. Screams filled the air while tables and chairs slid violently across the now cluttered dance floor.

"Surprise." Snow leaned down and whisper into Killer's ear. "Ma man you know um hard to kill. Um back from the dead." He pressed the hot gun barrel on Killer's cheek. He whimpered and grimaced in pain.

"Niggar you dead . . . . You dead man." Killer kept on saying as if trying to convince himself. He struggled to get up-holding his hands over the holes that were spewing blood out profusely.

Snow stood there silently watching as Killer's last dying movements unfold.

Angrily, Killer pushed the dead girl away from him. "Good for nothing Hoe; couldn't even protect me."

Snow shook his head in discuss-even dying, Killer was still a roach, caring for nobody but himself. He reached into his back pocket and pulled out his switchblade.

"You know Killer, um told that revenge is sweetest when you make it up close and personal; and nothing is more personal than the blade. And, revenge taste best when the one you are taking your revenge to knows that it is you. Payback is a motha-huh—Wouldn't you agree?" Snow said as the blade flicked open with a snap. The blade glistened and sparkled in the dim light of the club as though anxious to perform the task at hand.

Killer's eyes broaden as fear streaked across his face while he imagined what Snow's next move was. Now breathing more heavily than before, Killer tried desperately to get up and protect himself, or at least try to fight back-even while dying; but it was no use. Too many holes, too much blood lost, and no opportunity to catch Snow off guard for a second. No, he realized that he was doomed, and he now knew that he and his boys were doomed to die when they chose to bomb Peewee's house in an attempt to kill Snow. When you go to kill somebody like Snow, the rule is you're suppose to make sure that they are dead; see the body with your own eyes-the streets are very unforgiving to people who presume.

"When you get to hell, tell June bug them Snow said hello, and that his punk ass daddy will be joining him real soon." With those words, Snow, with a flicker, launched the blade across Killer's throat. Killer twitched and shook, and then fell limp with eyes staring horrifically back at Snow. He stood up, wiped the blood from his blade, and then turned and walked slowly towards the door.

"I suggest y'all make some withdrawals from Killer and his crew before the Popo gets here." He said softly looking into the scared crowd hiding behind tables and chairs as he exited the building.

They all rushed towards Killer and his men; pulling off their gold chains, watches, bill folds, and whatever else were in their pockets.

"You ain't gone need these where you going." One of the women said as she pulled off the six inch stilettos from the dead girl's feet. "Besides, they'd just melt down there sugar."

Snow eased into his car. "Every time you kill one roach, there is another one that you got to kill. Oh how I do despise them damn roaches and flies," said Snow as he cranked up his car.

Sirens blasting in the distance. fused with the sounds still echoing from Bobo's club. Snow, in his 65 Cheve, eased off silently into the night with June bugs daddy, Larry Slone, on his mind.

CHAPTER TWO

Princess sat lazily upon the couch staring blankly at the television, as music played softly in the back ground. She sipped on a glass of Mascato. Tears, filled with fear, eased down her face. She wiped them and cupped her head in her hands as she whispered a prayer. "Lord, I know that I am the last one in the world to ever call out to you, or even call your name for help, but I need you. Mama said that you were always listening, and that you cared for us all no matter what we've done," said Princess between hard sobs of rolling tears and anguished breaths. "Please protect Snow. He's just mad and confused and filled with revenge; and rightly so, cause you know them niggars ain't no good. They killed Candy and tried to kill Snow. So, please Lord bring him out of Bobo's safely. Maybe one day he'll be a wonderful vessel that you can use for your service; maybe me too, maybe both of us together. Please bring him out of there alive."

"Candy, if you can hear me girlfriend, I sure could use some pointers on how to be there for Snow." Princess spoke softly into the air while pacing the floor back and forth and twisting the ring on her middle finger nervously. "Girl, I'll put that other life behind me for Snow. You always said what a wonderful man he was-a girl just got to know how to treat him."

She kept pacing back and forth. Soon, she went back to the couch and sipped on another glass of wine while waiting. Finally, hours later, Princess fail asleep not really knowing exactly when.

A faint knock sounded on the front door. Princess was a light sleeper, so she heard anything out of the ordinary around her. Softly the knock sounded again.

She sat up knowing that it wasn't Snow because he wouldn't knock. It's his house. "Damn," she said faintly. "Who the hell can that be?"

Princess tip toed to the front door, and peeped out through the peep hole. An old white lady stood at the door knocking.

"Mr. Frank . . . . Mr. Frank." She uttered into the air. "Are you there Mr. Frank?"

"My god, white folks are so crazy. If he ain't home, what's he suppose to say, no I ain't home." Princess whispered to herself pressing her face against the peep hole trying to see the old woman.

"Mr. Frank . . . . Mr. Frank. I know you're in there; I here the music playing. I just have something to tell you of importance."

"Damnnnn." Princess whispered slapping her thigh while looking back at the stereo softly singing 'No woman no cry'.

"Mr. Frank . . . . Mr. Frank."

"What's this? The neighbor from hell?" Princess whipped. She decided to open the door for fear the old lady might call the police thinking that something had happened to Mr. Frank (Snow). She eased the door cracked opened. "Yes." She whispered softly peering from behind the door.

"Oh dear, excuse me." The old lady said bashfully. "I . . . . I . . . . I . . . . I am looking for Mr. Frank. Is he home?"

"Er . . . No mam, he ain't here," said Princess opening the door just a little bit more.

"Well who are you?" The old lady said rubbing the back of her neck uneasily, knowing full well that she had no business asking.

Princess wanted to shout out, "None of your damn business," but she didn't want to cause a stir with Snow's neighbors, knowing full well that he always kept a low profile. "Um . . . . Um . . . . Um . . . . Er . . . . his friend."

"His friend?"

"Yes mam, his friend."

"I never seen you here before." The old white haired lady said.

"Look hoe, I ain't never seen yo ass before either." Princess wanted to scream out, but instead, she softly said, "I just came to visit him. He's gone to the store."

"Where you from?"

"Nunya"

"Nunya? Where's that?" The old lady said looking sternly at Princess.

"Nunya damn business." Princess whispered under her breath.

"Huh?"

"I said, um from Philly." She shouted loudly making up the lie as she went.

"Mama." Another woman's voice rang out from down the hall-a young woman's voice.

Princess could hear footsteps coming towards them.

"What you want Joyce?" The old lady said looking down the hall.

"What is this . . . A family reunion?" Princess snapped under her breath.

"Huh."

"Nothing. I said um glad to meet all y'all."

"Who are you?" The young lady said wobbling up to the door breathing heavily. She was quite large and over weight.

Princess ignored her, and just looked at the old white lady.

"I said who are you?"

"She's Mr. Frank's friend from Philly." Snapped the old lady looking at the young lady like it was none of her business.

"What's your name?" The young lady said taking a sip from the glass of coke in her hand.

"Why, you gone eat me if I don't tell you." Princess whispered under her breath to herself.

"Huh." The old lady said turning away from the young lady and glaring at Princess.

"I said my name is Lorna."

"Lorna what?" The fat young lady asked between breaths.

"Why?" Princess whipped, now becoming irritated with the flow of questions.

"Oh, pay Joyce no mind. She is always so nosy," said the old lady with a big grin racing across her face.

"Me nosy? You."

"Er . . . I'd like to stay here and chat with y'all all day but I got something cooking."

"What? I don't smell nothing," said the old lady.

"Me neither," said Joyce.

"And I bet your ass can smell food a mile off." Princess mumble.

"Huh," said the old lady.

"I said I just started cooking it."

"Want me to help." Joyce said stepping forward towards the door.

"No . . . No . . . No . . . I got it. Now please, um busy, but we can talk later."

"How much later?" Joyce said smiling at Princess.

"When hell freezes over." Princess growled to herself.

"Huh," said the old lady.

"I said that we'll do it later sometimes."

"Well, tell Mr. Frank I need to see him when he gets in, ok." The old lady said while stepping away getting ready to leave.

"Ok, I'll tell him when he gets home."

"And I'll be back a lil later Lorna to taste your food." The young lady said as the glass gurgled from her sipping the last bit of soda through a straw.

“Ok hoe.”

“Huh,” said the old lady. “You sure do whisper under your breath a lot.”

“I mean . . . . I mean Joyce . . . . Yea Joyce.” Princess had a flash back for a moment. She slipped and addressed them like she said good bye to her girlfriends.

“I . . . er . . .” The young lady tried to say.

“Bye y’all.” Princess said, then closed the door in Joyce face.

“Come on Joyce. Must you get on everybody’s nerve that you meet?” The old lady said while pulling Joyce by the arm.

“But she is my friend.”

“Oh, hush Joyce. You just met Lorna-for peeks sake.” The old lady said while she and Joyce entered their apartment.

CHAPTER THREE

Snow, again with his dreads tucked up under his cap, and dark shades on, strolled unnoticed into a hole in the wall restaurant to use the bath room. He came out and sat at a table and ordered a cup of coffee. It was four in the morning. He sat and thought of his next move. His next move has to be planned, and planned well; for he knew that the word of him being alive was going to spread in the Hood quicker than hot food stamps during the first of the month.

"You can't kill them all son." Mr. Ire said as he slid slowly into a chair at the table.

Snow jumped-startled. Mr. Ire was the only one that could ease up on him like that. "Hey, what's up."

"You. Word of your deed earlier has spread through the city. You think that you can kill all of them roaches and flies?" Mr. Ire said rubbing his brow tiredly. "Snow, for every one of them that you kill, there is ten others that you miss; and if you get them all, there are still some young punks that's waiting to take their place."

"I know, but do you see what they did to my family? Do you realize that my sister Julia, uncle T.C and Uncle Poochie is gone, and ain't never coming back." Snow said angrily. "My little nephew that I never got to know, Peewee and his nurse, they gone Ire . . . . They gone! For what? Cause them roaches were scare to face me. Ohhhh, but they will . . . . They will very soon. You can count on it."

"Ok, you kill em all, then what?"

"I ride off into the sunset."

"Yea, right," said Mr. Ire. "You know it don't work like that. He that lives by the sword shall die by the sword."

"I don't need preaching to this morning Ire. Remember, I know what the good book says."

"Snow why don't you come and go with me, or go back with your grand mother and Old Joe."

"They still here?"

"Yea, they were hoping that you come back. She begged me to come talk some sense in you."

"Don't she realize that her grand child and great grand child ain't never coming back-never?" Snow said gritting his teeth and holding back the tears that wanted to ease from his eyes.

"Yea Snow, she is hurting, but she is going to hurt even more if her only grand son is killed too; and you know that

that's what's going to happen if you stay on this rampage." Mr. Ire paused. "Um just keeping it real with you son."

"I know Mr. Ire, but this is something I got to do. My very soul won't allow me to quit even if I wanted to."

"Well, I just wanted to tell you. Um going on with our original plan. Um going to take that money that you gave me, and start a new life down south. Maybe get me a little small place not for from the beach, and watch them young girls walk by wearing dental floss for a bathing suit." Mr. Ire paused for a moment amidst a lingering smile. "I know that I don't have but a few years left on this side, and I don't want to spend them watching roaches kill themselves."

"I am happy for you Mr. Ire. You've been more than a father to me. I can never repay you."

"You already have Snow."

"I just can't leave now. I got to get them. You know that. You know me like nobody else." Snow said glaring deeply at Mr. Ire.

"I know Snow, but I told Miss. Eleanor that I would try. They are leaving in a few days. Um leaving too. Um not going to sit around and watch you kill yourself. You're the son that I never had."

They stood up from the table, and hugged for a good long time while patting each other in the back. Some how, they both felt like this was their last time seeing each other. Tears screamed down Mr. Ire's face and lapped under his chin.

The cook came from the back with a load of dishes in his hands. One of the plates slipped and slammed to the floor.

Without a second thought, and hardly any effort, Snow dropped to one knee in front of Mr. Ire with both of his pearl handled pistols pointing at the scared stiff cook. The hammers now pulled back, bullets ready to send somebody, anybody to the graveyard without warning.

The cook just stood there frozen looking down the barrels of those two pearl handled nines like a scared dear caught in a hunter's spot light at night.

Mr. Ire eased his hand upon Snow's shoulder, for he knew that Snow's pistols had hair triggers. "Son, he's just the cook. Ease up Snow . . . . Ease up. He's just an innocent cook-that's all."

Snow eased the hammers back in place on the nines, still staring at the cook without blinking an eye.

"See, son you're too tensed."

"In the streets, he that presumes and assumes die soon. The streets are very unforgiving to those that presume. You know that Mr. Ire . . . . You know that." Snow said now looking sternly into Mr. Ire's face.

"I know Snow. I know. But everything has to do with time and a season. It is time to move on Snow. Everything points to your season in this place is up; and anytime a person operates outside of their season, they are operating in a curse, and doomed to fail."

"What!" Snow snapped.

"Um just keeping it real like we always have."

"Mr. Ire, sometimes a man has got to do what a man is supposed to do even when it hurts, or it is not his season. Why can't you understand that?"

"I do, but you're my son, and I just had to try; even though I already knew that you were not going to listen-it's a father's duty to try to save his son."

They talked for a little longer, hugged again, shook hands one last time and then Mr. Ire left.

Snow sat there for a few moments later, and then got up to leave. He looked over to the counter and noticed that the cook was still leaning against the counter obviously shaking. Snow walked up to the counter with the ticket to pay his bill. He laid it on the counter next to the cash register, then glared at the cook.

"Sorry," said Snow as he placed a hundred dollar bill under a glass, and then turned to walk away.

A waitress quickly ran to get the hundred dollar bill. "Ooh, thank you sugar." She said, grabbing the money.

"No." Snow whipped, glaring at her like a pit bull ready to strike. "It is for him." He pointed at the cook.

Nervously, the cook picked up the money and eased it in his pocket as though waiting for Snow to ask for it back. "Tha . . . . Thank you." He said.

Snow turned and walk out the door to his car.

"I don't ever want to get that close to going to hell again in my life." The cook said to the waitress.

"Why, how you know you were going to hell?" She said.

"Well, when you got two girls friends and an ex wife, and seven children all over the city, I think that is a pretty good chance of you busting hell wide open." The cook nervously said.

"Well, Willie you can change that. First get rid of them Hoes you got on the side cause all they want is your money; and take care of them lil seven rug rats you got all over the city." She said. "Then you might go to heaven, or at least not to hell-he might have a special place for dogs like you."

"I ain't no dog." Willie snapped. "You don't know me."

"Baby, if he walks like a dog, barks like a dog, acts like a dog, then he most likely is a dog."

Willie turned to go back to the kitchen.

"Willie, what the hell, you done pissed on yourself." The waitress said grinning. "He scared the piss outta you didn't he." She said, laughing hard while leaning against the cash register and staring at Willie's behind as he walked away embarrassed.

"You just go to hell Quitta . . . . Just go to hell." Willie said flipping her a finger.

"Now why I gots to go to hell. Ain't nobody scare the piss outta me. You ask me, grown ass men that pea on themselves need to go to hell." She loudly yelled after Willie.

"You crazy as he is Quitta."

Snow tried to stick the key into the lock on his car door. He dropped the keys on the ground, and then bent over and picked them up. When he stood back up, a big tall olive skin man stood right behind him. Snow could feel his eyes burning into his back. Quickly, he turned with his guns drawn pointing at the olive skin man standing behind him.

The man smiled. "You've become pretty good with those things you call guns-huh." He said, now folding his arms across his chest.

"What? You want to die tonight?"

"Don't think so Frank Junior, or Snow, or whatever you call yourself these days."

"Who are you?" Snow said nervously; thinking that maybe he was somebody from back home, for nobody on the streets knew him as Frank Junior.

"Why, does it matter? Somebody that's trying hard to die don't need to get to know nobody else." The man said picking at his fingernails casually.

Snow was amazed; for he had never pointed his guns at anybody that they didn't strike fear in. This man act as though he could care less-like Snow was pointing a play gun at him.

"How you know me?"

"What? Are you serious? I mean, come on Mr. Snow." The man said now looking at Snow with a big smirk on his face.

"I ain't never seen you before; I never forget a face."

"Me neither boy."

"What you just call me?" Snow eased the hammer back on his guns. "I don't have time for this; who ever you are."

"Frank Junior, I've known you for a long time-a very long time. Ok, ok sorry about calling you a boy. You people are so word sensitive"

Snow looked at him from head to toe-trying to measure him up. He had olive skin, long hair that draped upon his shoulders, and was about 6'11. He had big hands and big feet, but spoke softly and easily, like he was sure of himself-like he already knew what you were going to do before you did it.

"Ok . . . Ok . . . I'll bite. Who are you, and how do you know me?"

"Frank Junior, I've known you and your family from day one. I was there when you skinned your knee on the swing in the back yard; I was there when you and Julia sneaked down stairs late one night and got some milk and cookies that you all were not supposed to have, then poured water in the milk to make it seem still full." He paused, scratched his head with a smile, and said, "Yea Frank, or Mr. Snow. I've known you for all your little life."

"You ain't making no sense."

"I was there when you fail down stairs and Julia gave you a nickel not to tell your mother. Huh, I was even there when your father choked your mom to death; and I was there during his last moments of his life before they fried him. I sat right there beside him while he sat in that chair scared to death."

"Who are you!" Snow screamed still pointing the pistols at him.

"I am called Nathan." The man sneered. "You happy now man of clay?"

"I don't know no Nathan."

"You're not supposed to. I am not even supposed to be talking to you now, but somebody higher up thinks that you are worth bending the rules for . . . . Which I don't agree with, but who is Nathan for them to listen to."

"Are you crazy man? You ready to die?" Snow screamed.

"All I am here for is to tell you that you need to slow your role son; else you're going to join your parents and all the others before you. You've got to let some things go. In the end, revenge only kills you." He paused. "Trust me. I wish that you could talk to Alexander the Great-his young butt; or Mark Antony, or even . . . . well, you see what I am saying."

"Who the hell are you!" Snow screamed with tears in his eyes. Just then, one of the hair triggered pistols went off, sending a bullet sailing looking for a target-but there was none.

Snow opened his eyes, wiped the tears, then looked for the stranger, but saw no one. He was absolutely too close to have missed. He looked both ways down the darken street; looked up beside the buildings-nothing; and then he ran back inside of the hole in the wall restaurant that he had just come out of. There was no one except a frightened waitress and Willie the cook looking all buck eyed and scared.

"Where did he go?" Snow shouted to them.

"Where'd who go darling?" The waitress said.

"The man in the white suit with long hair. Where'd he go?"

"Baby, I saw you out there talking to yourself. I figured you just had too much Hennessey and too little sleep; so we left you along. I just stared at you and listened, but when you started to shoot . . . . Well."

"Damn, um tripping. Sure seemed real to me." He said as he pushed his gun back in his side. "I got to get outta here."

Sirens sounded in the distance. "What? Yall called the Popo on me?"

"It wasn't me dog . . . . It was her . . . . She . . . . She called the Popo." Willie the cook said pointing at the waitress.

"Damnnnn!"

"I didn't know what you were going to do-kill us or what; you out there shooting and talking to yourself. We don't know who you are, never seen you before, and won't remember you when you exit that door." The waitress said trying to get Snow to leave before the police arrived.

"Damnnnnn . . . . Damnnnnn . . . . Damnnnn!" Snow yelled as he ran out the door and jumped in his car and sped off into the night.

"Lord, all these niggars just done gone crazy round here." The waitress said looking at Willie the cook and slamming the cash register close.

"He . . . . He . . . He better be glad he left cause I was fixing to light into his ass." Willie stuttered looking at the door.

"Git your scary ass back in the kitchen."

"Why I was just playing like I was scare to fool him so I could catch him off guard."

"Yea, yea, you fooled him so until you pissed on yourself. Like to see you explain that one to your woman—playa." She said as she followed Willie back into the kitchen.

"No, um for real. I was thinking more of your safety than mine. If you were not here, shoot girl, I'd a been all over him," said Willie gesturing with his hands as he spoke.

"Yea, you'd a been all over him begging for your life. Thank god he didn't scare you any more; else you would have number two in your pants."

"Quitta, you didn't even have to go there."

"You right, my bag," said Quitta smiling. "You had him scared as hell; didn't you?"

"Well, I wouldn't go that far, but he knew I wasn't scare of him."

"Yea, right."

"You see how fast he left here don't you?"

While Willie was looking away going deeper into his lies, Quitta threw a pan on the floor. It sang out like a small gun had fired. Willie jumped under a table hollering as he went. Quitta just burst out with a hard laugh.

"I knew your ass was scared." She said brokenly amidst laughter. "What? You thought a shooter was under that table, and you were trying to get under there to protect me."

Willie just eased from under the table embarrassed and quickly walked back to the kitchen rolling his eyes at Quitta as he went. For the rest of the morning, she would burst out into laughter every time she saw Willie.

Later that day, Princess phone rang. It was Snow.

“Hello,” said Princess hesitantly.

“Hey girl.”

“Who is this.” Princess mused.

“It’s me Snow.”

Quickly she changed her expression, and spoke pleasantly into the phone. “Hey baby. How’d you get my number.” She asked. “I mean, I don’t care, and um glad you got it-just don’t remember giving it to you.”

“why.”

“Nothing, I don’t want to think that um losing my mind.”

“You’re not. I got it from a little bird.”

Princess chuckled. “Well, I want that little bird to always keep me in your view.”

“He does . . . . Hey can you come down to the court house for a minute?”

“Yea, for what.”

“I’ll tell you when you get here.”

“Are you in trouble?”

"Trouble is my middle name, but no, I am not in trouble. I just need you to come to the courthouse for a minute."

"Ok, I'll be there right away."

"Good." The phone went dead before she could say goodbye.

Princess wondered what in the world did Snow want with her at the court house, and why did he seem so secretive. She caught a cab to the court house and walked swiftly inside. Snow stood waiting for her on the other side of the metal detectors.

"Now what is it baby?" Princes said as she walked up to him.

"I know that this is going to sound crazy, but it's something I want to do, and you're the most likely person." Snow said hesitantly looking into Princess eyes.

"What sweetie. What do you want me to do?"

"Ah . . . . Er . . . . Uh . . . . Marry . . . . Marry me." Snow stuttered.

"Jesus!" Princess barely whispered.

"What."

"Um not going to tell you what I thought you just said."

"I asked you to marry me-what?" Snow said almost bewildered.

"Please ask me again so that I know that um not dreaming."

"Will you marry me Princess?"

"Yes, I will. Oh god, yes I will . . . . I will, but, but, why, why now?" Princess said as she slowly sat down trying to digest all of this wonderful news at one time.

"Cause I just want to be married at least once before I leave here."

"Leave, where are we fixing to go sweetie."

"No, before I leave," said Snow. "I am talking about dieing."

"What," said Princes jumping to her feet. "What are you saying Snow. I'll be a widow even before I get married good."

"I understand if you don't want to, but you're the only one that I felt I could feel comfortable calling a wife besides Candy."

"I do . . . . I do . . . . Oh god do I." She said. "But, why do you think that you're about to die?"

"Cause, I just don't think that this is a battle that I can win completely. They know that I am coming for them, so they will be ready."

"Let's just leave town Snow." Princess said, tears now swelling up in her eyes. "We can go where ever you want. I don't care; as long as um with you."

"You know that I can't do that." Snow grabbed her by the hand. "So, you ready to be Mrs. Frank Thomas Junior?"

"Frank Thomas Junior." Princess giggled.

"Snow, don't call me Frank; that's only for legal purposes." Snow said grimly as he looked hard at Princess.

"Ok . . . Ok . . . Ok . . . . You can call me Mrs. Dip stick if you want, as long as you are my husband."

Snow smiled, grabbed Princess by the hand and walked toward the justice of the peace. After it was all over, Princess couldn't stop smiling and gigging. She ran down the hall leaping and singing and speaking to every one that passed her way.

"I am married. Only in a America can a girl go from being a hoe one day, and married the next day."

"Please, please, no hoe. You're a lady now-my lady." Snow said with a smile.

"Ok."

"Go home and wait for me. I'll be home later. Still in a war."

"Snow, baby please take care of yourself . . . . please . . . . please . . . . please . . . . come back to me. Mrs. Snow."

Snow kissed her and walked through the doors headed for another war to be fought.

Princess walked down the sidewalk beaming as she went. Speaking and telling everyone that she was married . . . . Mrs. Snow.

CHAPTER FOUR

Snow turned the key in the door to his South side apartment. The door cracked open. He heard soft music coming from his bed room. Quickly, he snapped his guns forward-hoping that the old lady down the hall wouldn't decide to come out just now. The room was dark with fragrance candles flickering here and there. He eased into the darkly lit room-guns pointing straight ahead. Moving swiftly, but cautiously to the back bedroom, Snow breaths were short, and beads of sweat leaped from his brown. He turned the corner, and there was Princess lying asleep upon Snow's king sized bed-looking like a princess.

"Oh damn." He whispered to himself as he lowered his guns and tucked them back into his side.

Princess lay there, eyes closed, looking astoundingly lovely. Brian McKnight bellowed softly a love Ballard in the back grown. He then remembered that he was now married, and his new wife lay there waiting for him.

Meeting that Nathan fellow had blown Snow out of his zone. He started thinking that maybe the stress and all had started him to hallucinate. "That guy could not have been real." He thought to himself as he turned to walk away from sleeping Princess.

"Oh, you're not going to say hello to your wife sweetie," said Princess as she sat up upon one elbow and looked at Snow with those deep brown eyes.

"Uh . . . Er . . . . Well." Snow stuttered-overwhelmed by how so beautiful princess was lying there amidst the flickering candle lights.

"What, you mean to tell me that the cat's got your tongue Mr. Snow; my sweet wonderful husband."

"No . . . No . . . No, you just . . . . Just."

"Just what?"

She sat up and hanged her legs over the side of the bed while she sat erect and gazed into Snow's eyes-looking right down to his very core; the place that he kept secret and hidden from everybody-where only a few people had ever been allowed to go.

Her long black curls shined and glistened as they lay wantonly upon her smooth ebony shoulders. She had high cheek bones and deep dimples with a smile that would make even the average beast behave. She stood up. Her black very sheer Victoria Secret negligee lay upon her smooth sculptured body and dance upon her ankles as she took a step towards Snow. Her dark skin beamed like a leper's coat in the moon light just before it pounced upon its prey. Her figure was sculptured and tight. She was 5'10 with long tone athletic legs. Princess stood there gazing at Snow while he gazed back at her.

He hadn't thought about a woman in this way for so long-since Candy's death; a lot of bullet holes and dogmatic drama had engulfed his every thought. Now, here he was standing, for the first time in a long time, before a woman-his new wife—that simply took his breath away. He didn't like women that made him feel like Princess did; for it made him seem week and vulnerable.

Princess stepped into his arms; her eyes closed, her breaths short, her palms sweat, and her head swam. She couldn't believe that this was happening. She had dreamed of this day, but would never ever cross her best friend, and never even could imagine becoming his wife someday, but now, right now, she knew that this is what Candy would have wanted them to do-to be in love for however much time they had left together.

She moaned softly as she melted away into Snow's masculine arms. He whispered soft melodies into her ears that the very heavens had prescribe for only lovers to discern. He held her tightly and closely like he would never let her go.

That night, for the first time in a long time, the two of them journeyed to that place of love where neither day nor night nor moon's light exist; where time nor distance matter, that place where the world stops for two lovers to enter into that realm that was designed just for lovers-that place that every one wants to go, but only lovers can enter. The place where distance itself is but a grain of sand upon the seashores of time; that place where the flesh is but a pebble resting upon the mountain of love. This is where lovers go to hide themselves together from the toils and troubles of life; here, is where a man and his new wife becomes one.

He held her; his very soul promising never to let her go. He felt the gentle pounding of her heart as her breast let softly upon his chest. Now, he understood why a man like Julius Caesar would rather give up his kingdom than lose the love of his life-Cleopatra. He now could understand what Sir William Shakespeare was trying to convey when he penned his eternal epic of love-Romeo and Juliet; and now, no doubt, he understood the breathtaking splendor mixed with the excitement of forbidden love that King David must have experienced when he first peered over his balcony and secretly bathed in the awesome beauty of Lady Bathsheba.

As their breaths became one, fused by kisses of passion, a lonely tear drop streaked and ran down the side of his face. He knew that this couldn't last, but still he thanked the very God that he had heard his father preached so many sermons about. He thanked God for giving him the opportunity to cross the path of Princess (Lorna)-no doubt one of his very beautiful earthly angels that he had given him the opportunity to cross her path.

He held her tightly; she held him tightly; they moaned together as new love exploded and perfumed the air surrounding them.

The next morning, as the sun eased through their window and rested lazily upon the night table adjacent to the bed, Snow lay upon his side staring at Princess as she lay tangled in the satin sheets. Her eyes slowly blinked open; she could feel his stare upon her. She smiled; he smiled back.

"Hey you." Snow said gently rubbing his hand through her hair.

She smiled broadly and kissed his hand. "Hey."

"Princess is dead, don't answer to that name no more. Your name is Lorna; Lorna Thomas, my new wife, and that is what you ought to be called-by your name."

"Of course baby . . . . Of course."

"And no more Hoochie Mama dresses, or painted on jeans; you're a lady; my lady, and that means something," said Snow looking into Lorna's eyes. "You don't have to work nowhere, for nobody. I'll take care of you."

"Ok sweetie. I got to go get some things from my apartment."

"No." Snow snapped. "You live here now. Whatever you need, I'll buy it. Maybe you need to go shopping today and get you some new clothes."

"Well."

"Well, what? Is there anything in your old apartment that you just can't live without. Whatever it is, I'll buy it for you."

"No . . . . No . . . . Um good. I'll call my girlfriend and tell her that um gone and won't be coming back."

"Do you have some wheels."

"No, but I can drive your car if I need something, or catch the bus."

"No, my car is too hot, and too known. My enemies would shoot at my car even before they realize that it ain't me driving." Snow said now holding her hand. "I'll get you your own car. What kind of car you like?"

"Any car?"

"What do you want? You're my girl. You got to represent."

"Well . . . Well, I'd love to have one of those two seater Mercedes Benze." Lorna said slightly stuttering.

"What color?"

"Er . . . Red."

"Done. Give me a few days. I don't won't to ever see another man riding in your car."

"I . . . . I . . . . I"

"You hear me Lorna?" Snow whipped looking into Lorna's face sternly.

"Of course, why would I do something stupid like that?"

"Don't know, but understanding is the best thing in the world. I don't like my woman to guess about how I feel; and I don't want to guess about how she feels."

They talked way over into the day before Snow had to leave and go take care of some business. "I'll be back." He said.

"When," said Lorna.

"When I get back." Snow yelled back as he exited the door.

CHAPTER FIVE

Larry Sloan, June bug's daddy, sat slouched in his easy chair enjoying a lazy morning sipping on a cup of coffee. He sat anguished in deep thought as he reminisced about June bug, his dead son.

"I got him for you June; I got him." Mr. Sloan whispered in the silence. "That mixed up white boy Snow thought that he was invincible, but I showed his ass . . . . didn't even see it coming. Thought he was all that-hell, I wrote the book on gangster; he just read it."

He took another long sip of his coffee, closed his eyes, and sat back in his chair. He lived in a nice house on the other side of town away from the Hood, but his business ventures were in the Hood, he just thought that he was too good to live in a majority black neighborhood. He felt more comfortable around the white folks; in their neighborhood-even though his skin color was very dark.

Mr. Sloan, June bug's father, had tried desperately to show June bug the ropes, but June bug was arrogant and flashy-two things that didn't go together in gangster world; but he was proud of his son, for he was his only son. But, he knew for a long time that someone on the streets was going to punch June bug's ticket; so, he wasn't surprised when he got the news that Snow had killed him; as a matter of fact, Mr. Sloan expected it, for you didn't cross Snow, and lived to tell about it. He had tried to get to Snow to repay him for whatever June bug had ripped him off for. Then, word had spread on the streets how June bug had ripped Snow off, but June bug either too stupid, or too arrogant to disappear-either way, it caused him his life. Now, Mr. Sloan sat in his easy chair surrounded by white neighbors, and lavished the thought that now he could rest because he had finally gotten rid of the man that had killed his son; now, he can get back to making money. A big smile eased across his face while he exhaled deeply.

Suddenly, someone burst through his front door without ever knocking. He heard footsteps racing towards him. He threw his coffee to the floor; the cup smashed into a thousand pieces as it hit the floor and shot coffee everywhere. He raced towards his computer table where he had a gun taped up under it. He reached, grabbed, and turned to fire.

Just then, the running intruder tripped over a colorful Persian rug and fell crashing into the center table-breaking the top covering glass. He rolled on the floor trying desperately to get up.

Mr. Sloan had his gun pointed at the intruder-ready to send a bullet sailing. Just as he was about to pull the trigger, he recognized that it was his nephew, Lil John.

"Boy is you crazy?" Mr. Sloan shouted at Lil John as he scrambled to get off of the floor bleeding from the broken glass table that he had crashed into.

Lil John just waved his hand, asking for a moment to catch his breath.

"This had better be good," said Mr. Sloan.

"He . . . . He . . . . He is alive." Lil John struggled to say amidst hard pants.

"Who?"

"He . . . . He is alive," Shouted Lil John in excitement.

"Who is alive boy? You ain't making no sense."

"SNOW," snapped Lil John now pacing the floor back and forth-dripping blood everywhere.

"Snow? Here, hold this over your hand. You dripping blood everywhere," said Mr. Sloan looking at Lil John disgustingly.

"Man, blood on your pretty lil Persian carpet is the least of your problems," said Lil John. "Did you hear me? Snow is alive and out for revenge."

"Now wait a minute. Just hold on. You are mistaken. Snow is dead. Killer killed him."

"Yea, now that's the niggar that's dead for real-killer," said Lil John. "Snow shot them all dead yesterday-Killer and his boys, and their girlfriends."

"What?" Mr. Sloan said as he flopped back in his chair.

"Yea, his ass is still alive."

"Damn," said Mr. Sloan. "You sure."

"Hell yea. A whole bunch of niggars done seen him."

"Talk about hard to kill." Mr. Sloan moaned to himself. "Killer said that Snow was dead for sure-blown to pieces."

"That niggar lied to you. That's why he dead now; cause he believed his own lie." Lil John stuttered, dropping his head in worry.

"Damn."

"What we gone do?"

"Kill his ass again, unless he is a ghost." Mr. Sloan rubbed his beard and looked off into the distance thinking what to do next.

"Nawww dog, he ain't no ghost. Ghost don't carry machine guns and shoot up niggars."

"Why do you always have to use that word." Whipped Mr. Sloan looking menacingly at Lil John.

"What word?"

"Niggar. Why do you always refer to yourself and your race by a name that the white folks gave you? It is a name of degradation."

"I don't know, but I don't call them nigger-now that's what the white folks called us. I call them niggar-that's what we call each other."

"Nigger, or niggar, it's all crazy to me," said Mr. Sloan. "Anyway, I got to kill Snow again. Damn, he is worst than a fly on a horses behind."

"Well, um fixing to get outta dodge." Lil Wayne said, turning to leave.

"Yea, gone and run like a lil scared hoe."

"Call me what you want to . . . . scared . . . . hoe . . . . ,; I don't care, but my ass will be alive," said Lil John walking towards the door. "I mean, who gone be able to sleep knowing that crazy white boy looking for you; and you know he's not going to stop until you dead or he's dead."

BAM! BAM! BAM! A 45 automatic thundered in the air, sending three bullets searching.

Lil John hollered, and jumped to the floor holding his hands over his head.

"See, Snow don't have to kill you," said Mr. Sloan, pointing the 45 in the air. "I can. You probably need to fear me just as much or more than you do Snow. You don't run out on me. I'll kill your black ass quicker than Snow."

"What . . . . What . . . . What's going on down here?" Mr. Sloan's wife screamed out as she stumbled down stares staring at Lil John lying on the floor. "Larry, what are you doing?"

"It's alright baby; just gone back up stairs. We just handling business."

"What is this-the OK Corral?" Mrs. Sloan said with discuss while turning to go back up stairs. "Lord, what are the neighbors going to think?"

Lil John, shaking terribly, struggled to get off of the floor. "Man, is you crazy?"

"Yea, and don't ever forget it."

"Damnnnnnn!" Lil John moaned.

"I know . . . . I know . . . . You feel like the rat in the middle of two hungry lions; not knowing which one is going to eat you first." Mr. Sloan chuckled while putting the gun into the table drawer.

"You know you crazy man."

"Yea, but what you need to do now is find out where Snow is, so we can strike him first."

"Yea . . . . Yea . . . . ," said Lil John walking out the door.

“Keep me posted.” Mr. Sloan hollered after him. “And don’t make me come looking for your ass.”

Lil John just waved his hand in the air amidst anger, and walked on towards his little two seated sports car; got in, and sped off.

“Damn, um a have to get rid of him and Snow, but Snow first then Lil John to cover my tracks.”

Mr. Sloan poured him a glass of Scotch, sat back down in his comfortable chair, and pondered his next move to get rid of Snow and Lil John.

CHAPTER SIX

Old Joe and Eleanor sat on the side of the bed. Old Joe held her tightly in his arms-stroking her back as she wept upon his shoulder. They were still amidst grief; still horrified that someone would try to kill all of them just to get her grand son-Frank Junior. Julia, her husband, and her little boy, T.C and Poochie, Dr. Pee Wee and his nurse were all gone-murdered by someone trying to kill Snow.

All the funerals, the crowd, the grave yard, and the constant tears had left Eleanor and Joe sick and emotionally drained.

"We got to get on back home honey," said Old Joe. "As much as it hurts, we still gots to go on and live."

"Ohhh Joe, but what about Frank Junior." Eleanor moaned between hard sobs of tears. "I don't want to bury him too Joseph."

"He's a man Elly. He has to choose to live or die here. He can come back home with us, or stay here; it's his choice, and you can't make it for him." Old Joe said, holding back his own tears. "My boys are gone, and ain't never coming back. For years, they lived among killers, murders, and robbers in prison-very mean men, and they survived, and then get free and come out here and get murdered by some crazy thug over nothing. I don't get it; I just don't get it. I know that God has a plan, but what is it?"

"We must go on Joseph-trusting as we go forward. Even holding our pain in our bosom wrapped in tears, we still must go forward." She lowered her head as she spoke-now barely above a whisper. "Even leaving Frank Junior behind in this wretched place, we must go forward Joseph; for if truth be told dear, you and I don't have much longer. Our days are but few left together; so, I'll pick myself up and love you until the Lord calls one of us home. I am hurting now Joseph, but I'll be alright. I got through my son killing his wife, and then dying in prison, and I'll get through this too-this too shall pass."

"I know baby. You the one that gives me strength Elly," said Old Joe. "Yea, we gone trust God as we always have. He's never failed us yet. He is still in control in spite of the madness."

While they sat there consoling one another, a light tap sounded on the door. "Yea." Old Joe yelled to the door. "Who is it?"

"It's me."

"Me who?" Snapped Old Joe.

"It's me Ire."

Eleanor leaped to her feet and ran to the door, hoping to hear something about Frank Junior. She swung the door open; Old Joe standing beside her with his hands in his pockets.

"Come on in Ire; come on in," said Eleanor.

"How's y'all been these last few weeks?" Mr. Ire asked, staring at them. "I know, it's a stupid question, but I knew nothing else to ask."

"We're fine Ire," said Old Joe.

"What about Frank Junior?" Miss Eleanor interjected.

"Snow? . . Er . . . Frank Junior, he's fine ma'am. I just saw him yesterday."

"Thank God," said Eleanor with a sigh of relief.

"But, you know Snow. He's on this revenge thing come hell or high water, and you know, y'all, I can't say that this time I much blame him." Mr. Ire said hesitantly rubbing his beard and walking through the door. "Cause if I was just a lil bit younger, and a lil bit stronger, I'd be right along side him, killing them roaches."

"But he's going to get himself killed Mr. Ire." Eleanor burst out.

"Miss. Elly, I wouldn't count Snow out too fast. A whole lot of roaches been trying to kill Snow over the years, but he always came out on top . . . . And, I suspect that this time will be no different."

"So, what brings you here this morning?" Old Joe asked.

"Just checking on y'all, and . . . . er . . . . I . . . . I would like to go back with y'all," said Mr. Ire gesturing with his hands. "Of course, I wouldn't be on y'all cause I got my own money. I'll get me a place. Snow straightened me before the bomb. I am set. I can live anywhere, but you alls like the only family I got."

"You want to move back to our town?" Ask Eleanor.

"Yea, I do."

"We'd be glad to have you Ire-real glad," said Old Joe.

"Yes, we would." Eleanor chimed in. "Now what about my grand son?"

"Well, you know Snow, he's going to get even, or die trying."

"That's what um afraid of-the latter."

"I told you, Snow is not easy to kill. You'll see. I just decided to move on while I can. I tried to talk Snow into it too, but he said that he would be on after he finishes this business."

The three of them sat upon the bed, and talked and talked, and talked until late into the night. They even laughed a little here and there. For the first time since the bombing, Eleanor felt that they would be alright in spite of their lost.

Old Joe beamed and grinned when he spoke of T.C and Poochie. After all of the stories, and ventures, Mr. Ire felt like he knew all of them. They had a lot to get past, but some how and some way, they would; with God's help, they would.

CHAPTER SEVEN

Atop an old raggedy motel several blocks away, Snow, with a high powered rifle, leaned against a leaning sign, and looked through his binoculars at a night club that he knew Mr. Sloan frequented. He had been there since 7 pm; it was now 1am in the morning. He was tired, cold, and hungry, but he knew that Sloan would come sooner or later; and he was willing to wait for as long as it takes. He blew into his hands-trying to warm himself, then looked hard again at the club through his binoculars.

"Never seen such a hard headed piece of clay just bent on destruction . . . . Well, no I lied . . . . One called by the name Hitler was too."

Startled, Snow whirled around so fast until he dropped his rifle. Quickly, he reached into his side and flung out his pearl handled pistols and pointed them in the direction of the familiar, yet unsuspected voice.

"Hello, Mr. Snow. Nathan at your service." The man in the white suit playfully gestured to Snow.

"What? You don't have nothing to do but follow me around all day? You in a hurry to die dude?"

"No, but it seems you are."

"Why are you getting involved. It's not your war."

"I told you, I've been involved since you were a child."

"ohda ba ge" A voice hissed out of the darkness.

"Caove." Nathan answered the voice without taking his eyes off of Snow. "Ma po hyon?"

"Lomed," answered the voice deeply out of the darkness.

"Lomed ma?" Questioned Nathan, now turning and looking into the darkness

A man in a black suit stepped out of the darkness. Snow now pointed one gun at Nathan, and one at the stranger in the black suit; Tailored dressed, with an air of dignity about him.

"Eene ebodah." The man said bowing slightly to Nathan in respect.

"Huh!" Nathan laughed.

"Er, I hate to break up this Spanish reunion, or whatever language y'all speaking, but, will y'all take that somewhere else." Snow said looking from one to another while waving his guns at them.

"It is Hebrew if you must know; though, we do speak Spanish also," said Nathan. "Kay pausa Morrow?"

"Nada." The man in the black suit replied back to Nathan.

"I don't care," said Snow.

"We speak all languages."

"Speak English then, alright."

"Alright," said Nathan.

"Why are you here Morrow?" Nathan asked the man.

"I am always here Nathan; you know that. My people called me about this piece of dirt that you've so much interest in." He said staring off into the distant darkness. "Why is that prince Nathan?"

"I just do as I am told. You know that. Unlike some people," whipped Nathan, now amidst anger.

"Truth be told Nathan, I am merely an opportunist-that's all. You know that. I only do what I am allowed to do." He said. "Now you, on the other hand, wait for things to happen—How boring!!"

"Look, I can give a flip about either of you. Why don't y'all take y'all's beef somewhere else?" Snow shouted at the two of them. "Or, I am going to have to put a bullet in both of you."

"Stupid dirt." The man in the black suit mumbled.

"He's more ignorant than stupid," said Nathan.

"He's just dirt . . . . Clay . . . . Dust. Look around you Nathan. It's everywhere. Why waist your time protecting something so plenteous, and it's not even gracious enough to be appreciative."

"What do you mean it? I ain't no it. I am a he. You lil freak in the black suit. What's this Halloween?"

The man in the black suit took a step toward Snow. Nathan stepped in front of him. "Don't do nothing stupid Morrow."

"I don't plan on it. I was just fixing to tell Mr. Snow that Mr. Sloan will be arriving in about 45 minutes." He said as he stepped back into the shadows. "Make sure you breath slowly, relaxed, then squeeze the trigger Mr. Snow. Remember, I am on your side. Holler at you later prince Nathan."

Just like that, the man in the black tailored suit was gone just as suddenly as he had appeared. Nathan stared at Snow, trying to read what was Snow thinking.

Snow turned around, looked through his binoculars once again at the club-all was quiet. He turned again to say something to Nathan, but he too was gone. He pondered what was happening; who were these men with him tonight, and who was this Nathan guy that seemed to be so interested in him. Snow scratched his head and sat on the roof with his pistols still in his hands, and thought hard until, in the midst of the cold, he fell asleep.

CHAPTER EIGHT

Julia, Snow's sister's husband Johnny's family was still in town too, but only three of them—Uncle Leroy, Aunt Louise, and Big Ma. They too waited and hoped that they would hear something about the killer. Uncle Leroy, a man of the streets, had gone to several of the night clubs to find out the real story; and learned what the story was behind the bomb, and how utterly dangerous Snow was.

They sat in the lil hole in the wall restaurant and ate a late dinner while talking. As usual, Uncle Leroy was well saturated with alcohol.

"Well, we got to get on back home," said Aunt Louse. "God knows um a miss my nephew."

"Me too child," said Big Ma.

"Can I help y'all," said the waitress, Quitta, as she walked up to the table. "What would y'all like to drink."

"Scotch and water for me please." Uncle Leroy joked.

"We only have beer."

"Leroy, haven't you had enough?" Aunt Louise sang out.

Big Ma just shook her head in discuss, and looked at the waitress. She read her name off of her name tag on her blouse. "Qu . . . Quitta is it?"

"Yes mam."

"Pretty name baby," said Big Ma. "I'll just have a glass of sweet tea. Is it nice and sweet baby?"

"Yes mam-real sweet."

"Well, we'll all have sweet tea baby."

"Ok."

"I don't want no tea. Brang me a beer honey." Uncle Leroy shouted hitting the table with his fist.

"Must you always make a scene Leroy?" Aunt Louise said softly.

"He can't help it baby. A fool is going to be a fool no matter where he goes," said Big Ma going through her purse.

Uncle Leroy just looked at her sternly, and then shook his hand at her. "Um a let you have that one Big Mary. Um a let you have that one, but don't try it again."

"Oh hush up Leroy," said Aunt Louise.

"No, let him go; don't stop him. jump over this table if he wants, I'll cut him so many times, he'll look like a piece of Swiss cheese."

The waitress laughed, trying to hold it.

"Yea, you real funny Big Ma . . . . Real funny," said Uncle Leroy, looking around the restaurant. "Anyway, as I was about to say, I'll have a beer."

"What kind?"

"Baby, it don't even matter-even if it's rubbing alcohol. Just bring him whatever you want."

"You gone let your grand ma talk to me like that Louise?"

"What? I'll cut her too; she know it." Big Ma whipped with a slight smile.

The waitress, Quitta just kept on laughing. She dropped the ordering pad on the floor, and then bent over to pick it up. Uncle Leroy gazed at her behind as she bent over.

"Look at him, just a dog too-a drunk and a dog. Girl you show can pick them." Big Ma said to Aunt Louise as she rolled her eyes at Uncle Leroy.

"Leroy!" Aunt Louise shouted at Uncle Leroy.

"What? What? I was just admiring her uniform that's all."

"Louise if you believe that, I got some beach front property I want to sell you in Utah."

"See, I wasn't gone say nothing, but since you trying to crack on me, ain't no beach in Utah." Uncle Leroy said laughing hard.

"That's the joke dummy; if she believes your story, then she'll believe that there is an ocean in Utah. You so slow." Big Ma smiled broadly as she spoke to Uncle Leroy. "You need prayer baby."

"I don't need jack." Uncle Leroy shouted.

"No, not you; Um talking about Louise. She need prayer to put up with you."

They sat and enjoyed their dinner while uncle Leroy downed several beers.

CHAPTER NINE

Willie and quitta sat quietly and gazed into the crowd as they danced to the beat of an old Michael Jackson song. Willie bobbed his head up and down-wanting to dance. Quitta just sat there trying to look as cute as she could for the men that passed by her table.

"Quitta." Willie shouted above the throbbing music.

Quitta just kept staring into the dancing crowd.

"Quitta." Willie shouted a little louder.

"What." Quitta shouted back.

"Let's dance."

"For what."

"What you mean for what," said Willie hutching his shoulders and extending his hands. "People just don't come in this place to look you know."

"I do." Quitta snapped.

"I want to make this an exciting date."

"Nigga this ain't no date." Quitta said rolling her neck and looking sternly at Willie.

"Oh, it's like that-huh."

"Uh, Yea," said Quitta. "We just kicking it as friends."

"You know what, you are sooo ful of . . . ."

"What . . . . What . . . . Um just trying to keep it real." Just then, Quitta started to say something when her mouth fell open as she stared at the bar beyond Willie's shoulders.

Willie turned to see what had gotten Quitta's attention. His mouth too fell open. He knocked his drink over trying not to openly stare.

There, standing at the bar, was Snow. His golden blond dread locks lay lazily upon his shoulders glaring in the dim club light. He sipped on a glass of Hennessey and stared menacingly across the scattered crowd. Wearing a black leather suit and a black turtle neck with a diamond cross glistening around his neck, he looked like a fine lethal weapon standing there waiting to be fired upon somebody, anybody. Most, privately stared at Snow; not believing that he was still alive; others got on their cell phone to confirm to someone else that he was really alive.

Snow knew the activity around him. It was his plan to show himself, for he realized that his time of ambush and surprise had passed; so he wanted his enemies to know and be warned that he was alive and well, and on his way to punch their clocks.

"Lord ham mercy Quitta; we got to get the hell outta here girl." Stuttered Willie. "That crazy white boy ain't nothing but trouble."

"Now see, that's what um talking about."

"What?"

"Yo ass want to turn and hall ass before you even know what's going on. Ma man is supposed to protect me. How you gone protect me running like hell all the time."

"Who . . . . Who . . . . Who was fixing to run?" Willie asked with a nervous sheepish grin across his face.

"Don't even trip like that. You know you were fixing to dip."

"Um just thinking about your safety; trying to get you outta here first. Cause you already know I will whup his ass if I have to." Willie said trying to look like a thug.

"Nigga please"

"What?"

"See, that's why we don't date and you're not my man cause I need a man that's willing to stand up for me. I mean, I would fight with him," said Quitta. "But yo ass is ready to run at a drop of a dime."

"You want me to go up there and slapped that thugged out nigga?"

"He's a white boy."

"Well, you want me to slap that white boy to show you how much I care about you," said Willie standing to his feet.

Suddenly, a tray fell over off the bar and slammed to the floored echoing a loud noise of shattering glass though out the bar.

Willie dived to the floor with his hands covering his head.

Quitta leaned down and softly whispered in is ear. "Mr. bad ass, that was just a tray falling on the floor . . . . And you gone protect me?"

Willie eased his hands down from his head and looked at the few people staring at him and chuckling to themselves as they whispered about him. He was filled with embarrassment.

"You can get up now superman." Quitta shouted as she eased back in her seat.

Willie stumbled up off the floor, and looked over at Quitta sitting there sipping slowly upon her glass of white wine with a big smile on her face.

"I was . . . . I . . . . I was just trying to collect myself fore I jumped on his ass."

Quitta rolled her eyes and took a big sip from her glass.

Snow still stood at the bar unmoved by the events. He glanced at Willie lying on the floor, and kind of smiled because he recognized them from the hole in the wall restaurant. He sat his drink back down onto the bar; rolled his dreadlocks back upon his shoulders; straightened his coat; rubbed his hand slowly across his diamond necklace, and casually walked towards Willie and Quitta's table.

"Well, spider man you've done it."

"What?"

"Mr. dreads is on his way to us." Quitta tried to whisper with her hands over her mouth.

"What?"

Willie turned and saw Snow walking sternly towards their table. "All hell, what we gone do? He's coming this way Quitta. What we gone do?"

"You gone protect me ain't you?"

"You out your damn mind girl. I ain't fixing to die for my mama," said Willie as he squirmed in his seat.

Snow eased up to the table. Quitta looked into his eyes with a big smile plastered on her face. Willie just sat there trying to act calm.

"Y'all sure have a way of attracting attention to yourselves don't you," said Snow glaring at Quitta with a crooked smile across his face.

Quitta thought that his crooked smile was sooo sexy. She rubbed her hand slowly across the back of her neck, then ran it slowly down the front of her satin low cut blouse, and rested it upon her exposed cleavage.

"And you have a way of scaring the hell outta people." Quitta said as she slowly moistened her lips sexily with her tongue and looked deeply and sternly into Snow's ocean blue eyes.

Snow smiled.

"You like scaring people don't you?" Quitta asked as Willie sat there still trying desperately to look calm.

"No, obviously it doesn't work on you-huh." Snow said barely above a whisper.

"Take a lot to scare me babe."

"Is that right?"

"Yea, but I like thugs," said Quitta as she took another slow sip from her glass.

"So you think I am a thug-huh?"

"No, I didn't say that; but I do find you soooo damn sexy."

"You don't bite your tongue do you?"

"No, why should I. I like keeping it real."

Willie cleared his throat and shuffled in his seat.

"What?" Quitta said looking at Willie.

Snow smiled broadly. "I think you're sexy too sweetie," said Snow as he turned and walked away from the table. "I'll be seeing you later."

"I hope so." Quitta shouted after him.

"You can count on it." Snow hollered back without changing steps or looking around.

"Why you go dissing me like that?" Willie asked leaning into Quitta.

"What?"

"Flirting like that right in my face. You gone make me snap up in here," said Willie picking up his glass.

"Er . . . Snow." Quitta hollered out towards the door, knowing full well that Snow had exited the building.

Willie jumped, turned around, almost tilting over in his chair, and gazed at the door.

"Funny Q; very funny. You gone make me whip that imitation black man one day."

"Anyway."

"What's wrong with me Q?" Willie asked now serious. "You already know how I feel about you."

"Nothing wrong with you Willie, but you know what I am looking for, what I want in a man." Quitta paused for a moment and thought. "Above everything else Willie I want security; both physical and financial . . . . And you don't have either. Not trying to diss you; it's just the way it is."

"But I ain't going to be working at that restaurant forever you know. I got plans," said Willie. "What happened to a woman standing by a man and helping him be something? See that's what's wrong with y'all crazy ass sistas. You want it all right now . . . . with your angry black woman attitude."

"Just go to hell Willie . . . . Go to hell."

"Why cause um keeping it real with you now? While you trying to wait for this night in shining armor, or for this mixed up white boy to save you, um not gone be waiting for you forever you know."

"Ok, whateverrrrr."

"No, um serious. You know how I feel about you. No, I ain't no fighter, and um just a short order cook in a hole in the wall restaurant, but I ain't gone be there always. You waiting for him to come along, and um already here. I love you, but all that white boy gone do is use you and beat your ass then toss you to the curve."

Quitta just sat there, now looking at Willie sternly as she listened-knowing full well that Willie was telling the truth; truth that she didn't want to here; truth that she was denying, for she had been used so many times before, and had been beaten many times by dogs-too many slaps to count. Her eyes swelled with tears, for raw truth often hurt.

"Look, um sorry," said Willie grabbing Quitta's hand and squeezing it softly, affectionately.

"No, you right. I just been a hoe that attracted no good dogs; always thinking that um in a relationship when to him um just a booty call." A lone hurt filled tear ran down her face as she dropped her head.

"No Q, I was out of line. I just care about you so much. Yea, um usually scared as hell, and will run quick, but I do still love you. Even when I don't want to, my heart won't allow me to feel nothing else, even when I know I don't have a chance in hell with you."

"Let's go Willie," said Quitta as she leaned forward and kissed him on the forehead. "I know you care Willie, and you're probably right, but I just want . . . . I want . . . . I don't know what I want . . . . I am so confused most of the time Willie."

"Well, I will wait for as long as it takes. I love you Q, and I promised that I'll always be there for you-scared, and we might have to run sometimes, but I'll always be there waiting for you."

Quitta smiled, grabbed Willie by the hand and pulled him close as they walked towards the door.

"I know Willie. You are such a good friend."

"But I want more than friendship."

"We'll see."

Willie walked Quitta to her car. A note was stuck to her windshield. Willie grabbed the note, read it and balled it up and through it on the ground.

"What is it?" Quitta shouted as she stooped down to pick the note up.

It was from Snow; saying that he'd like to meet with her tomorrow around 7pm at the uptown restaurant in the Hilton.

"Yes!" Quitta screamed into the air with excitement.

"You ain't fixing to go meet him and make a fool out of yourself. Did you here anything that I said in there," said Willie opening Quitta's car door and motioning for her to get in. "Now go home and I'll see you tomorrow at work."

"Nigga you ain't my man. Why you tripping. Yea, I think the white boy is sexy as hell."

"You just got jungle fever."

"Whatever."

"You don't even know his name?" Willie snapped.

"Yea I do. His name is Snow."

"How you know that?"

"Don't worry, I know."

"Well, I was just about to jump on his ass. He better be glad he walked away when he did."

Quitta burst out laughing.

"What?"

"See, that's why I like you so much cause you so funny." Quitta said between laughs.

"Um serious Q, don't go up there. In the end, all he's gone do is use you . . . . But, you're going on anyway, aren't you."

"Yep, sure am."

Willie just waved his hand at her in discus as he walked away and got into his old car and sped off.

Quitta just kept smiling while getting in her car holding the note to her heart, and feeling like a little excited teenage girl about to go on her first date.

CHAPTER TEN

Lorna scrambled around the apartment going from one room to another trying to get dressed. She was dressing and trying to do her hair-all at the same time.

"This wife, and good girl stuff is all so new to me. Dear lord how am I gone pull this off-taking all I got not to cuss that ole fat hoe out down the hall." Lorna whispered to herself while pulling a hot iron through her hair. "A lady doesn't do that; she just bow politely, and nod her head hello, then stab her ass in the back later on." Lorna talked to herself in the mirror as she got dressed.

Finally, she finished dressing, and headed for the door with her sun dress on and pointed stilettos; and a sun straw hat that hollered fashion to passing on lookers. She opened the door to step out, and there standing at the door about to knock was Joyce-the young fat lady from down the hall. She was munching on a cookie with crumbs scattered across her collar.

"Oh, hey Lorna," said Joyce.

“Hey,” Lorna whipped back.

“What you doing?”

“Um about to run some errands.”

“For what?”

“Look, what do you want? I am about to go and you can’t go with me.” Lorna snapped irritantly.

“Joyce . . . . Joyce,” hollered the old lady from within the apartment down the hall. “Joyce where are you.”

“Down here mama talking to Lorna.”

The white haired old woman eased out of the apartment wiping her hands upon her apron as she came. “Why hello Miss Lorna.”

“Hey . . . Um . . . . Um . . . . kinda busy right now. I got to go handle some business.”

“Did you tell Mr. Frank what I said?” The old lady said walking up still closer. “My, my, don’t you look wonderful. Pretty as a peach.”

“Thank you, and yes I told him.”

“Well, what’d he say?”

"He said that he'll see you soon. Now look, I got to go; I am late for an appointment." Lorna said as she brushed pass them.

"Can I go with you?" Joyce screamed out-cookie crumbs falling out of her mouth.

"Hell to the knawl," mumbled Lorna softly.

"What you say?" The old lady said pulling Joyce by the arm to guild her into the apartment.

"I said not this time." Lorna said rolling her eyes.

She walked into the public garage to search for the car that Snow had bought her. "I wonder what he bought me. Probably something just to get around in, but I don't care as long as I got him."

She looked from one car to another, trying to figure out which was hers; then she remembered that she had the remote key button in her hand. Snow had left it on the table before he left. She held the button high in the air and pushed. Suddenly a loud beep filled the air for a fraction of a second. She hit it again; and again a loud beat filled the air. She kept on hitting the button, and following the sound there of; now she saw the flashing tail lights when she pushed the button.

Lorna walked up to the car. It was a shining black convertible SL 500 Mercedes with black interior trimmed in gold with a card laying on the driver's seat.

"Yes . . . . Yes . . . . Yes . . . . That's what um talking about . . . . Yes . . . . Yes . . . . Thank you Jesusssss!!" She shouted as loud as she could in the parking garage. "Ohhhh, my Boo is off the chain. Lord ham mercy; I got to sit down."

She opened the door, grabbed the card off the seat and sat down to catch her breath. The card simply said, "hope you like it. If you don't, we'll pick something else." She started to cry as she laid her head softly upon the steering wheel.

"Now I know why you were always so happy Candy." She said as she looked up towards the ceiling. "He's a good man, and sweet too." Slowly she ran her hands along the leathered dash board, and sheep skin leathered seats. She let the top back and eased out of the garage and crept down the street as though she was in a parade.

She just had to slowly stroll through her old neighborhood with her top back and watch the on lookers gaze at her and wonder who she was. She stopped at a red light, and ran her hands gracefully through her hair as she waited for the light to change. Beonce was belting from the radio loudly.

"Hey sweetie, give the brotha a ride . . . You won't regret it." A young fellow hollered out at her. Lorna looked over at him sternly through her Ray Ban sun glasses-never smiling, just staring indignantly at him.

"Oh, it's like that huh." He yelled out as his friends laughed at him and edged him on.

The light turned green, and Lorna eased on, now passing BoBo's hole in the wall club. As she turned down Martin Luther King Street, a woman yelled out to her.

"Princess!" The lady screamed out with a high pitched voice. "Princess . . . . Girl is that you?"

Lorna pulled over and noticed her girlfriend from the streets. It was Valerie-everybody called her V. V was the one that watched Lorna's back on the streets when she was Princes. They were like family.

V ran up to the car, and Lorna jumped out. They hugged screaming as they twirled around and around laughing with excitement, and glad to see each other.

"Girl, where you been? I thought you were dead. Jesus, I am glad you're alive," said V smiling broadly.

"No, I ain't dead honey. I am still kicking; just kicking a lil differently now a days." Lorna said while playfully turning around like a runway modal. "What's been up with you?"

"Same ole same ole girlfriend. Niggas still crazy, but a girl gots to do what a girl gots to do to makes them ends. You feel me."

"Yea girl, you know I feel you if nobody else do. I do. We all paper chasers-truth be told."

"So, how you kicking this?" V said pointing at the Mercedes and Lorna's new look.

"I just went straight girl; that's all"

"That's all?"

"I found somebody that was worth it; somebody that knows a woman's worth," said Lorna with hints of tears in her eyes.

"I wish, but I am happy for you, real happy for you girl." V started to say something else, but before she could, two shots pierced the air. By habit, V and Lorna hit the ground.

A young man came trotting by them as fast as he could. Boom . . . . Boom . . . . Boom . . . . An old man followed him trying to run, and shooting at the young man as he went.

"Come back here you damned thug. Come back here!!" The old man hollered after the young man who was fastly disappearing down the street.

He stopped, panting hard in front of V and Lorna-hardly able to breathe. He held the gun up, aimed and pulled the trigger, but all he heard was empty clicks from his gun.

"Damn, out of bullets, but um a get his ass. I know who that punk is. Um a get his ass; y'all watch and see." He said as he turned and limped away.

"See girl, why I gots to get off of these streets. All these niggas done gone crazy," said V. "Look, let's meet in the mall down town at Macy's tomorrow. You better get outta here with that fancy car before you get jacked."

“I feel you girlfriend-thanks. What time you want to meet?” Lorna said as she scrambled to her feet and quickly got in her car.

“let’s say about one.” V shouted as she brushed the side walk dust from her jeans.

“Ok, it’s a plan darling. I’ll see you tomorrow at one . . . . Kiss Kiss!”

Lorna sped off, squealing tires as she went. V rushed off into one of the adjacent little stores to get off the streets until things cooled off.

“What? Y’all niggas never seen a Mercedes before?” V snapped as she passed by some men leaning against the wall looking at her as she passed by.

“Oh it ain’t the Mercedes baby; it’s them kicking jeans you advertising.” One of the men snapped back with a gold teeth glaring at V. “Apple bottom-that’s what um talking bout.” His friends all burst out laughing as they gave each other high fives.

V just waved them off, and kept moving.

CHAPTER ELEVEN

Lorna eased into the building; took her stilettos off and tried to tip toe pass Joyce and the old lady's apartment. Suddenly, she heard the chain upon the old lady's door rattling as somebody tried to open it. She dropped her stilettos to the floor and eased her feet in them-no need trying to tip toe now, she thought to herself.

"Thought I heard somebody come in the building," said the old lady as she flung the door open and stepped out. "You know, Miss Lorna, we have to watch out for one another around here."

"Yea . . . Yea," said Lorna waving her hands in the air and faking a smile.

"Is that Miss Lorna Mama?" Joyce said, trying to squeeze pass the old lady.

"Yea, now get on back inside. Miss Lorna's busy. Get back inside." She said while pushing Joyce back inside.

"I'll see you later Miss Lorna . . . . Ok." Joyce yelled.

"Yea, yea . . . whatever." Lorna whispered to herself. "Hopefully, I'll see you first, then you won't see my black ass."

Lorna struggled to put the key in the door knob, for she was still shaken and nervous from the shooting in the Hood. Suddenly, the door clicked and eased opened.

Standing just beyond the threshold, looking sternly with penetrating ocean blue eyes, was Snow. He motioned for Lorna to come in. "You alright?" He hissed barely above a whisper.

"Yea . . . Yea, um . . . . Um good." Lorna hesitantly said. "What's wrong?"

"What were you doing on Martin Luther today?" Snow said softly, then took a small sip from his glass of Hennessey.

"Er . . . . Ah . . . . Ah . . . . Ooaaa." Lorna moaned to herself. "How'd you know I was on Martin Luther today?"

"Cause those are my streets. Nothing happens on my streets without me knowing about it; and even sometimes me overseeing it." He pushed his golden dreadlocks off of his shoulders, eased his glass upon the table, crossed his legs, and patted the couch next to him-motioning for Lorna to sit down.

"I . . . . I . . . . But I." Lorna struggled to say.

Snow eased his hands upon her lips softly and whispered, "I know you had to show your girlfriend your new life style-I feel you, but stay out of the Hood. Princess is dead; you're a lady now."

Lorna became agitated, for she never liked a man trying to tell her what to do. "Wha . . . . What? Oh you gone tell me what to do and where I can go, and who I can see-huh?"

"No, if I got to always tell you what to do, I don't need you," picking his glass back up, and sipping slowly, Snow laid back onto the couch-gazing into Lorna wondering eyes.

"Well, what's all this about? If you ain't trying to tell me what to do Snow."

"Not a meeting babe; just an observation-that's all."

"Just because I got out, don't mean that I should turn my back on those that are still in the Hood struggling to get out. There are a lot of good black men and sistas that's trying to do the right thing; trying to raise their families, and teach their sons to be men and their girls to be ladies. They don't have other options. The Hood is their home, so they have to make it work." Lorna clearly irritated, for she loved her people and her Hood. "The problem with many of us blacks is that when we make it out, and start living better, we try real hard to forget where we came from; and start thinking that just because you live on the other side of town with the white folks, you better than those that are still struggling in the Hood."

"Ah . . ." Snow tried to interject beneath a slight smile.

"No, I owe it to my brothers and sistas to go back and help somebody else to make it out, and at the very same time, I should try to make the Hood a better place cause everybody can't get out, and some don't want to get out because it's all that they know," said Lorna sitting on the edge of her seat staring at Snow as she spoke. "Ain't nobody gone make things better for us; we got to do that. So, I am going to see what business I can open up in the Hood-maybe a lil community center for girls and boys to get off the streets; I got to do something."

"That's what I like about you; you're an independent thinker, and you care about others. I think you ought to do what you've said-help others . . . . I could see that in you-that's what drew me to you," said Snow as he eased into Lorna, planting his lips upon hers. "I just want you to be careful out there." He said without hardly moving his lips from hers.

Lorna just moaned pleasantly, and threw her arms around Snow's neck and pulled him in closer . . . . She's finally found a man that will support her vision of helping and assisting others . . . . Usually, all the good men are taken.

CHAPTER TWELVE

Mr. Sloan sat amidst his company of, what he called, common interest folks. He puffed slowly on his long cigar and sipped from his tall glass of wine. Sitting there with their three piece suits, and diamond up, they all looked like successful distinguished business men.

"So gentlemen, what we gone do about our common problem?" Mr. Sloan said as he grimaced from the strong smoke from his cigar. With his legs crossed and his hands resting in his lap, he spoke directly as puffs of smoke eased to the ceiling.

"What you mean we? Seems to me you got the problem dog. Snow not looking for us. We didn't send a boy to kill him." One of the men said sternly while gazing hard into Mr. Sloan's face. He leaned into the table when he spoke-as though ready to strike at an enemy.

Mr. Sloan uncrossed his legs, gently placed his cigar in the ash tray, blew the last bit of smoke out of the corner of his mouth, and said, "Look you two cents hustler; you were nothing before me. Now, you're making a lil money, and you think that you all that. Well, let me tell you something Mister. You survive because of me. When I want to shut you down, you shut down." Mr. Sloan said gritting his teeth. "Snow is all of our problem. When he stops my business, he stops yours. He is bad for business-period." Mr. Sloan slammed his fist hard on the table-knocking over the glasses and a bottle of Scotch.

The men around the table kind of shuffled in their seats and mumbled among each other. Right now, life was good for them, but they knew that none of them wanted to make Sloan an enemy. He was not the same since Snow killed his son June Bug. He went from being a smooth business man to being a ruthless killer chasing that green paper. Too, they also knew that they couldn't afford to show fear at any level; for when Sloan knew that you feared him, you became his prostitute-and he slapped you around when he wanted to-just for sport to sometimes entertain those that stood by that he wanted to impress.

"Why you tripping, and acting all crazy like that . . . . Slamming your fist on the table. You act like some hoes sitting here, or you talking to your wife." One of the men sitting at the other end of the table smoothly moaned while glaring hard at Sloan.

Suddenly, Mr. Sloan picked up a glass and flung it hard at the pimp while screaming out some choice profane words. The man dodged and reached his hand into his coat pocket. One of the men sitting next to him pressed his hand inside his coat so that he could not bring it out.

Mr. Sloan rested one of his hands behind his back upon the handle of his pistol. He stood there with a smirk smile on his face, as if daring the man to try and draw his gun.

"Now hold on gentlemen . . . . Just hold on," said one of the other men sitting at the table.

"That's what um talking about," said another.

"That old man better recognize. I ain't no punk; and I ain't his hoe," said the man slowly pulling his hand from his gun. "So he better come with respect. What? Snow done made you crazy man. You scared of that white boy?"

The man kind of smiled and eased back in his chair.

Without warning, Mr. Sloan picked up the bottle of Scotch and threw it hard against the wall-smashing it into a thousand pieces. The other guess in the club started to run from their tables. The owner of the club ran towards Mr. Sloan, but before he got there, Mr. Sloan held up his hand and motioned for him to stop.

"Don't worry Don, I'll pay for any and all damages." Mr. Sloan said without ever taking his eyes off of the bold young man.

"Alright Sloan, but cool it man," said Don the owner. "Alright."

"Ok . . . Ok . . . Just letting off some steam; that's all," said Mr. Sloan as he dropped back into his chair and exhaled hard, then took a big gulp of from his glass of wine.

All the regular customers had cleared the place. Don promised them a free meal and drinks upon their return. He looked over at Mr. Sloan and shook his head in discuss as he picked up one of the knocked over chairs.

"Don't make no sense." Don moaned to himself.

"Well, um out of here . . . Old man is crazy," said the young man getting up from the table. "He gone get all of y'all killed. Watch what I say. Gone and mess with that crazy ass white boy. He's crazier than old man Sloan."

"You're pathetic." Mr. Sloan yelled after him.

"Yea, say what you want old man, but me and my hoes a be coming to your funeral."

He turned, straightened his coat, tilted his hat at the other men at the table and began to walk away.

Bam! Bam! Bam!

Mr. Sloan sent three bullets sailing into the young man's back. He hit the floor hard like a sack of rocks. Blood covered his back and eased out of his mouth and nose. He lay upon the floor in his fine tailored suit and designer alligator shoes twitching and struggling to breathe.

"What the hell," said Don the owner as he crutched down behind a table.

"Don't worry, I got this." Mr. Sloan said as he walked up to the young man lying on the floor now in a puddle of his own blood. "Shut all the doors and lock them, and close all the blinds."

Nobody moved.

"Did y'all hear me!!" Mr. Sloan screamed to the top of his voice while waving his pistol around at every one.

Everybody jumped up and started closing the blinds and locking the doors.

"Ain't nobody seen nothing; right?" Mr. Sloan shouted. "Right."

"Right." They all moaned one after another.

He took another sip from his glass, sat it down, and then grabbed a napkin off of the table and began wiping his gun down as he walk to the bleeding pimp, then stood over him.

"Now, whose funeral was it you and your hoes were going to playa?" Mr. Sloan said while holding his hand to his ear acting like he was trying to hear what the dying man said. "I can't quite hear you dog with all that blood in your mouth . . . . What . . . . What . . . . what you say? You sorry . . . . Nawl dog."

Bam! Bam! Bam!

He sent three more bullets smashing into the dieing man's back.

"Damned fool, ought to know you don't walk away from an argument with your back to your enemy-any fool knows that . . . . But, I guess this nigga didn't," said Mr. Sloan staring down at the now dead young man.

The man no longer twitched or moved at all. He just lay there as blood streamed from his bullet holes, his mouth and his nose.

Mr. Sloan turned, and walked back over to the table where the other startled men sat nervously.

"Anybody else want to object, or got something smart to say," said Mr. Sloan glaring menacingly at them while gritting his teeth as though he hoped that one more of them would object so he could send them to hell too. He had killed many men, and the young man was just another among many-they all knew it.

"What we gone say?" One of the men said, looking around the table. "Ain't no more fools here."

Everybody forced a chuckle uncomfortably, trying hard to pacify Mr. Sloan.

"Ok, so now let's get back to business," said Mr. Sloan dropping hard back in his chair. "Will y'all get that dead niggar outta here; and somebody clean up that mess. Don, I got you. Just send me the bill."

Some waiters and a few of the men in the bar rushed over and grabbed the dead young man and walked out back with him while the dish washer and others scrubbed up the blood off the floor.

CHAPTER THIRTEEN

Old Joe and Miss Eleanor sat in a swing upon the porch, cuddled up in each other's arms. The cool autumn breeze swept up over the shivering colorful trees and rested upon the chilled porch where the swing squeaked and churned as Old Joe and Miss Eleanor sat in the midst of silence and pondered upon yesterday and hopes for their future. Billowing gray clouds eased lazily across the somber unyielding sky. Old man winter whispered and tickled their ears of his pending return. Fallen leaves raced across the brown grass, mingling with others that were yet falling. God, the master artist, had painted the earth with hues of red, brown, gold, and yellow; for the earth is his constant canvas. A few naked trees stood masterfully erect and shameless as the last of their leaves deserted them and floated to the waiting cold dry still ground.

"Joseph, I miss them so much," said Eleanor weeping softly as warm tear drops streaked down her cold face.

"I know sweetie; I know."

"Will we ever get over this? I think about it often, and sometimes I dream of Julia and my great grand son."

"Elli, some things we never just get over; we just learn to live with them," said Old Joe fighting back his own tears.

"As a parent, some things just don't seem natural. You're not suppose to outlive your children-not suppose to have to burry your own child," she said, eyes now filled with tears. "It's just not natural."

"Yea, I know Elli . . . . I know."

"I had to bury my son, his wife, my grand daughter, and my great grand child; not to even mention my good adopted boys T.C and Poochie. I didn't know that I would have to endure so much pain and suffering." Miss Eleanor said now looking down and wringing her hands as she spoke ever so softly. "I never experienced that kind of pain before. You know that you love your child, but you have no idea how much you really love them until they are hurt, or, oh god, when they are lying there cold and stiff in that casket. I've never felt more pain than when they were lowering my babies' caskets down into the ground . . . . Oh god . . . . dear Jesus . . . . It hurts; it hurts sooo badly. That hole in the ground is the last time that you will see them again. It is so final. My heart have just been torn out and thrown away . . . . Oh Joseph . . . . Oh Joseph."

Old Joe just grabbed her and held her tightly, and allowed all of her tears to flow upon his shoulder. "I know Elli; I know. You ain't supposed to bury your child. They suppose to outlive you."

"Dear God, take care of Frank Junior. I just can't bury another child. I just can't."

"It's gone be alright," said Old Joe, still trying desperately to hold back his own tears-trying to be strong for Eleanor.

"Why won't he just come home Joseph? Killing those men that killed his family won't bring them back."

"Elli, he's a man, and he makes his own decisions. We just have to ask the good Lord to watch over him. The bible says that he knows how much we can bear, and that he won't put no more on us than we can bear," said Old Joe holding her tightly; his own tears now streaming down his face and dropping onto her shoulder. "That means sweetie that if we are going through it, God has already given us the strength and courage we need to make it through it. Yes, it hurts like hell, but we'll get through it-this too shall pass."

A gust of wind whistled and hurled a herd of leaves upon the porch. The barely clothed trees in the yard shook and shivered amidst the whispering wind, while the last bit of sunlight glimmered just behind the distant grey mountains as shadows of night loomed closer and closer-just waiting for the last bits of day light to hide beyond the disappearing mountains clothed by the on coming night's misty fog.

"Let's go inside darling. My bones getting chilly out here now."

"Ok . . . . Ok . . . . I guess I am just a big cry baby tonight-huh?" Eleanor said as she tore herself away from Old Joe.

"No . . . . No . . . . We supposed to cry. God put that in us so we could release some of that pain that we carry every day. If we didn't cry, we'd burst light a pipe under pressure," said Old Joe. "You hear some of these folks at funerals telling folks don't cry don't you gone make yourself sick, and I be thinking to myself that if they don't cry they gone make themselves even more sick."

They got up and walked inside holding hands as they went. Eleanor walked straight to the bedroom to refresh her makeup. She always tried to look her best at all times for Old Joe. While she was gone, old Joe grabbed a CD from beneath the TV and put it in the CD player; suddenly, Marvin Sapp bellowed-piercing the silence as Eleanor walked back into the room.

"Never would have made it." Sapp echoed through the room. "Never would have made it withoutttttt you."

Eleanor just fail to her knees crying hard and bitterly. Old Joe rushed over and grabbed her.

"Um sorry Elli. I thought the song would help."

"It does Joseph; it does. It's what I need to hear because the only way that we're going to make it through this is by the help of the Lord. Marvin Sapp is right. He is ministering to us Joseph. The only way that we're going to make it through this is through him-Our Lord and Savior."

"Praise God . . . . Amen Elli."

CHAPTER FOURTEEN

Quitta sat impatiently at the table of the fine uptown restaurant waiting on Snow. She sipped upon her third glass of very expensive wine. Snow had already called ahead and ordered the wine for the hour, and told them to give her whatever she wanted and as much as she wanted, for as long as she wanted. He was intentionally late. Well, he wasn't late at all; as a matter of fact, he had beaten Quitta to the restaurant, but he just stood in a private undisclosed place and watched her. Snow was always very calculative. He tried not to be surprised by people, and always liked being in control-which is why he personally didn't drink, smoke, or do drugs. It was his business, not his pleasure.

Quitta was quite tipsy by now, and becoming quite irritated by Snow's lateness.

"Either his ass don't value my time, or he think that um just stuck on him; either way, his ass is sadly mistaken." Quitta whispered to herself. "Might as well have me one of those big expensive T bone steaks on him while I am here."

She motioned for the waiter as she took the last sip of wine from her glass.

The waiter rushed up. "How may I help you mam?" The waiter said as he refilled Quitta's glass.

She was now more than a little tipsy. She giggled a little bit here and there as she spoke to the waiter.

"Tell me kind sir, what is the most expensive wine that you have here?" Quitta said with a slight slur.

"Well, Madam, we have in the cellar, Romanee-Conti 1990. It is 5800.00 a bottle," said the waiter as he cleared his throat.

"Bring me a bottle of that stuff Bro," said Quitta toasting the waiter with her glass as a little giggle leaped from her mouth.

"Are you sure Madam?"

"Quite; as a matter of fact, bring me two. I am a lil thirsty tonight," she said. "teach his ass to be late on me." She whispered to herself.

"Right away Madam."

The waiter called the Head waiter over to him, and told him Quitta's request. "Hold on a minute before you go get it."

He went over to Snow's undisclosed private place where he just watched Quitta.

"Sir, the Lady wants two bottles of Romanee-Conti 1990. It is 5800.00 a bottle. She has already had a bottle of our special House wine. It is 100.00 a bottle, and she has ordered the 200.00 T Bone meal, which brings your total to 11,900.00, which counting gratuity, it shall be over 12,000.00." The waiter paused for a moment, and then continued. "Do you wish to stop her?"

Snow looked angrily at the Head waiter, and said, "Hell nawl, do I look like 12 grands will hurt me? I told you to give her what she wants, as much as she wants, and for as long as she wants it. Did I stutter, or was there something unclear about what I said." Snow snapped softly at the waiter, trying not to bring attention to his position. "You know what. Tell the owner I said that I would like to see him. Tell him Snow asks to see him."

"Oh please Mr. Snow. A thousand pardons. I didn't mean to offend you. I shall do as you asked, and I or my staff shall never question you again . . . . Please." The Head waiter said nervously as he looked down at the floor-staring humbly away from Snow.

Snow just sat there for a minute as he pondered to himself-rhythmically tapping his index finger on the end of the table. He softly moaned, "Ah . . . . Uh . . . Ok, no offence; just give the lady what she wants."

"Right away sir." The waiter quickly disappeared into the cellar, and returned with two bottles of Romanee-Conti 1990, and placed them on Quitta's table-opening one of them and filling Quitta's glass.

"Damn! What? You freshly squeezed this-or you had to fly somewhere and get it," said Quitta amidst snickers.

"No Madam, only the best for you."

Just then, Snow eased up to the table, and motioned for the Waiter to leave.

"Oh hello Mr. come when you get ready." Quitta snapped.

"Ok, I am sorry, but I had business to attend. Let me make it up to you." Snow politely whispered as he eased into his chair and stared into Qutta's big brown eyes.

"Oh, you think you are soooo smooth-huh," said Quitta taking a big gulp of wine from her glass. "Well, see this wine here; it is Ro . . . . Rom . . . . Ro, oh it's some kind of expensive wine. It's so expensive until I can't even afford to call its name." Quitta laughed hard at her own joke.

A crooked smile eased across Snow's face. For some unexplained reason, he liked Quitta. Somehow she sooth the beast in him and gave him some kind of cool peace deep inside of him.

"Well, couldn't you have called a sista or something . . . . Men! Um always being stood up . . . . What is it? Do I have a sign on my forehead that says please make me wait, or don't show up at all." Again, Quitta laughed hard at her joke.

"Um sorry."

"Yea, I get it." Quitta said, taking another sip of her wine. "Lord, you are such a Man."

"Pardon," said Snow as he eased his chair closer to Quitta's.

"Pardon? I said that you are such a Man; cause only a man will do something so crazy and then expect it to be alright . . . . such a Man."

"Ok, I am a man, but isn't that what you want? Isn't that what every woman wants-a man."

Quitta just stared at him deeply with her now red wine riddled eyes. "You . . . . You . . . . You are changing my words on me. I didn't mean it like that. I meant that a man can be such an unconscious, uncaring, unloving, and uncommitted ass."

"Ooh . . . . ouch." Snow said playfully while squeezing Quitta tightly around the waist.

She purred like a little kitten; closed her eyes, and held on tightly to her glass of wine. "God, I am such a fool; cause as bad as I want to say no, my body is screaming yes." She whispered to herself while taking another big gulp from her glass. "I am being such a woman!"

She stood up from the table and said, "I am fixing to go."

Snow stood up and held her hand affectionately. "Well, let me take you home."

"No, my driver will take me home."

"Your driver?"

"Yea, I caught the bus." She said, and again burst out laughing at her own joke.

Snow laughed a little also, and then pulled Quitta up close to him, and laid a kiss softly upon her lips.

She stared into his eyes, wanting to pull away, wanting to slap his face, wanting to scream at him, but she couldn't; her heart refused to allow her to. "I am being such a woman; such a woman."

"So what are you supposed to do?"

"I supposed to slap your face and tell you to get lost as I strut out of this restaurant."

"So are you?" Snow whispered softly into her ear-gently biting on her ear lobe.

She felt his warm breath caress her ear-forcing her body to yield without her consent. "No, I want to, but I cant . . . . No, I don't want to. You make me feel so good-too good for my own good." Her eyes rolled back in her head; she realized that she was fighting a losing battle. Her body had never felt this way before-screaming at her to let go and forget about all those other dogs who had broken her heart before, forget about the many lonely tears she had shed, and the hurt that she constantly carry in her bosom, and believe once again that all men are not dogs, and that there is still a good man that's just for her.

She picked up her glass of wine, took another big gulp, and turned to walk away; then suddenly, fell back, unconscious into Snow's arms.

Snow simply smiled, picked her up and carried her to his car.

The next morning Quitta awakened at the Ritz Carlton hotel; in the Pent House suite where the elevator opens up to your room. It had windows from one end of the wall to the other; you could look for miles out over and beyond the city. It had a sunken living room with custom English furniture, and hand crafted mirrors everywhere. Your feet nearly disappeared in the carpet with every step. The bedroom was filled with mirrors, even one on the ceiling. An old Larry Gram song played softly in the back ground-One in a million. Quitta's bed was covered with red satin sheets. A lone rose lay upon the fluffy pillow beside her, and three dozen long stem roses lined the wall at the foot of her king sized bed.

"Ooh . . . . Who." She exclaimed in wonder as she looked down at what she had on. A shear white Victoria Secret negligee adorned her curvy body. Her head swirled with a million thoughts and questions.

A note propped up against a bottle of wine stood upon the End table. She reached over to get it.

"Ohhhh god." She whispered to herself. She had a head ache. "Too much wine."

Quitta grabbed the note. It read, "I thought that you might want to keep this bottle of 5800.00 Romanee-Conti wine that you couldn't finish last night. Oh, and there is something for you on the dresser in an envelope-go buy you something pretty . . . . And, I fired your driver last night-I got you a lil something in the parking deck. Just give them this ticket, and they'll bring your car to you."

Quitta held the parking ticket in her hand in disbelief. Her head swirling from last night wine and today's dreamy racing thoughts.

"Oh god, um dreaming . . . . Yea, that's it; um dreaming, and um a wake up in a minute." She whispered to herself as she remembered that the note said that there was a little something for her on the dresser in an envelope. Quitta walked over to the dresser, and opened the envelope. There were thirty one hundred dollar bills stuffed inside with another note that said, 'I've already called your job and told them you wanted off today'.

She fell back onto the bed crying softly in amazement. Larry Gram still humming One In A Million softly in the background; then she remembered her gift in the parking deck. She jumped to her feet and ran to the closet.

"Where are my clothes?" She exclaimed sliding the closet doors open. She didn't see her clothes, but what she saw was a Gnocchi outfit and a pair of Jrenee shoes to match.

"Lord have mercy!" Her knees got weak; she had to sit down a moment. "Please, if um dreaming, please don't let me wake up."

She slid into her Gnocchi outfit and Jrenee shoes, and readied herself to leave, and then remembered that she had no purse, therefore, no license.

"Shoot, where did he put my purse?"

She ran over to the dresser and opened the drawer. She gasped when she saw the Reed Krakoff two-tone ribboned large tote hand bag. Last month she was looking through a women's magazine when she saw some Reed Krakoff hand bags-they were at least a thousand dollars. All of her stuff was inside the bag. She became nervous and sick to her stomach from excitement.

She got on the elevator and went down stairs and gave the parking attendant her card. She waited impatiently wringing her hands as she walked back and forth with her Gnocchi outfit on and sporting Jrenee shoes and a Reed Krakoff hand bag to match it all.

"Girl, I like that bag and those shoes. Lord have mercy. Where you get them from?" A passing lady squealed at Quitta as she passed by.

"Er . . . . Ah . . . . Uh . . ." Quitta couldn't get a word to come out of her mouth.

"I wouldn't tell nobody either girl, but know for sure, you are sharp girlfriend."

Quitta waved her hands with a big smile and tried to say thanks, but nothing still wouldn't come out of her mouth.

Just then, a new candy apple red BMW eased up to the front of the hotel. The attendant came to Quitta and said, "Your car mam." He handed the keys to her and swiftly walked off to the next waiting patron.

Her head was now spinning more than ever. She could not believe this. She eased in the car with the Black and red interior. Quitta drove slowly around the block, stopped and started crying-crying hard. She couldn't believe what was happening to her, and why. She hadn't done anything for him, or to him; so why was Snow being so good to her . . . . Why . . . . Why . . . . Why??

CHAPTER FIFTEEN

Snow sat a few blocks down from the hole in the wall restaurant where Willie and Quitta worked. He squatted peering around the corner waiting for Mr. Sloan and his passé to come out. He was filled with anger blood boiled and rushed through his veins like steam from a locomotive. Memories of his sister Julia pervaded his mind like a strong east wind that's been blowing for far too long. Deep down in his heart, he really wanted it all to end tonight with Sloan and his posse', but he knew all too well that it never ended that easily-never.

He looked down at his pearl handle 9mm pistols, and made sure that they were loaded and ready. He patted both his pockets to make sure that he had six extra clips-three in both pockets. "That ought to be enough for them roaches." He whispered to himself.

"Well, when you really think about it, will you ever have enough bullets? Will you Mr. Snow?" A voice echoed out of nowhere.

Snow whirled around; guns pointing in the direction of the voice.

"You are always pointing those things at me. My . . . My, you are such a hot head," said Nathan, still wearing his white suit.

"Lord have mercy." Snow exclaimed.

"Now that's what um talking about," shouted Nathan with his hands raised high in the air.

"You sure in a hurry to die. Look, I don't want to hurt you man, so please, will you just go away. Go bother somebody else that will like your popping up out of nowhere, and your corny advice . . . . Please."

"I just do what I can Frank Jr. I just do what I can."

"And don't call me no Frank Jr." Snow shouted hard at him, and then turned around quickly to see if anyone else heard him.

"Ok . . . . Ok, Mr. Snow, but don't you think that this is a little crazy going against Sloan and all of his men in there with him?"

"No, I don't think that it's crazy at all; if you ask me." A voice sounded out of the darkness and walked into the edge of the light.

"No, nobody asked you." Whipped Nathan with a hint of anger.

"What? Y'all just like having a family reunion with me," said Snow, glaring from one to another. "You, in your white suit; and you, in your black suit. Don't y'all have some other clothes."

"Damned dirt, always more concerned with the shell-how unworthy." The man in the black suit said as he angrily stared at Snow.

"Morrow, I would ask you what you doing here, but I am sure it would be futile. Like bad whether, you always come at a bad time." Nathan kind of smiled as he spoke to Morrow.

"I just like going where the action is; and, my people tell me that there's going to be a whole lot of action on this very corner in just a little while." Morrow whipped, folding his arms.

"They got that right," said Snow. "So if y'all good ole boys don't want to get hurt and mess up your clean lil suits, I suggest you move on in a hurry cause when Sloan comes out of that place, there's going to be bullets flying everywhere."

Nathan laughed.

Morrow just rubbed his hand casually across his face and said, "Foolish piece of dirt. See, that's what bothered me Nathan; always having to be concerned about this worthless unclean hunk of dirt that don't appreciate you no how."

"Will y'all just go down the road and argue. If you ask me, both of y'all are crazy as hell."

Morrow flinched quickly and turned Snow's way with out stretched hands and lower brows.

In an instant Nathan stood between Snow and Morrow-smiles now gone, looking more than serious.

"Now Nathan, old friend, you know I don't roll alone." Morrow chuckled lightly as he smoke with an air of sarcasm. He clapped his hands, and there was movement in the shadows-much movement. He chuckled more loudly this time than before. "You want to risk yourself for this unworthy piece of dirt; who will never appreciate you, and whose concern is only with the things that he can see."

"You only impress those that you lead Morrow. You know full well that I too am never alone." Nathan waved his hand through the air, and the entire block lit up like it was mid day outside. The movement in the shadows squealed and leaped back into whatever shadows they could find.

"Ok . . . . Point taken; thought you were slipping Dog." Morrow said with an air of joke.

"You know better than that. Our battles run long and deep. I've forgiven you, just haven't forgotten you," said Nathan.

"look, what is this? Come onnnn guys. Damn, how am I going to ambush somebody with you two out here trying to show off. I don't know how you do it, but will you please turn off some of this light . . . . Please??" Snow shouted at Nathan and Morrow.

Nathan snapped his fingers, and the light returned to its original self.

Again, shadows moved in the outskirts darkness.

Nathan raised his brows and looked sternly at Morrow. He began to slowly raise his hand again.

"Ok . . . . Ok . . . . Ok," said Morrow. "My crew just like action. You know that Nathan."

"If that is what they want, then I shall give it to them." Nathan raised his hand higher.

"Ok . . . Ok. Just hold on." Morrow waved his hand towards the shadows, and they dispersed-leaving only the darkness that was suppose to be. "But, I am not going anywhere. Things are about to heat up I think." He said smoothly as he pointed at the entrance of the hole in the wall restaurant.

Mr. Sloan and his passé was coming out of the front door, talking loudly and laughing as they came.

"Look at them, think that they don't have a care in the world," said Snow, cocking his 9mms. "But um about to give them something to care about."

"You sure you want to do this Frank Junior?" Nathan shouted, trying to change Snow's mind.

"I told you Snow, not Frank Junior. They blew up Frank Junior with his sister and nephew," said Snow, now walking out from behind the corner-out of the shadows.

"Yea, he is sure." Yelled Morrow. "Let's get this party started."

Both guns raise high in the air, Snow's pearl girls sent six bullets sailing searching for a target. All of them hit their mark-not one missed anyone. Six men lay painfully bleeding on the pavement. Sloan reached for his gun.

"Go ahead try it." Snow shouted, walking up closer to Mr. Sloan-guns still pointing at him while aware of the scrambling men on the ground.

"You got me. What can I say?" Mr. Sloan said coolly. "Good help is so hard to find wouldn't you say Snow." Mr. Sloan said looking at the men on the ground.

"Nawl, I work alone."

"Mind if I take my last smoke?"

"Yea, you breathe too hard and um a send you to your son June Bug." Snow hissed.

A burst of anger streaked across Mr. Sloan's face as he remembered that Snow had also killed his son June Bug, and now looked like he was about to be killed by the very same man-Snow.

"Damn," exclaimed Morrow.

"Be like that sometimes. Don't always turn out the way you planned it-huh." Nathan said now grinning with approval.

"Well, I ain't through yet," said Morrow softly nodding his head in the air as though giving a cue.

"Neither am I," said Nathan, preparing for Morrow's next move.

Standing there, with the gun pointing at Mr. Sloan, about to kill the man that had killed his family, Snow felt a sense of relief ease upon him as he began his descent to squeeze the trigger on his most dangerous enemy.

Suddenly, out of the corner of his eyes, without taking his eyes off of Mr. Sloan, Snow saw something large and black coming fast his way. He jumped out of the way just in time to be missed by an out of control mustang. It slammed into the wall in front of Mr. Sloan, knocking him against the wall, and knocking his gun from his hand. It slid under the car.

Snow hit the ground hard and rolled to a stop. His guns still cocked and in his hands.

"Damn." Mr. Sloan snapped loudly as he watched his gun slide up under the car. He took off running.

Snow jumped to his feet, and started running after Mr. Sloan-shooting as he ran.

"Damn, this is better than the movies; wouldn't you say Nathan," said Morrow as they followed shooting Snow as he chased after running Mr. Sloan.

Nathan just rolled his eyes at him, knowing full well that Morrow had a lot to do with tonight's event.

Mr. Sloan kept running; Snow kept shooting. Bullets whist passed Mr. Sloan's head as he turned the corner running as fast as he could.

Finally Snow reached the corner, and turned widely around the corner just in case Mr. Sloan were there waiting. It was dark, and it was a dead end alley. He knew that Mr. Sloan was back there some place. The alley was deep and filled with garbage and tossed out furniture and things nobody wanted or cared for.

Snow eased down the alley, one step at a time; step by step . . . . inch by inch . . . . Step by step . . . . inch by inch . . . . He darted around a fallen refrigerator with guns pointing-ready to fire, but no Mr. Sloan.

"Ooh, this is so exciting to see a piece of dirt finally annihilated. Man, I just love my job Nathan," said Morrow.

"Sure you do." Nathan whipped back, keeping his eyes peeled on Snow's every move.

"I know . . . . I know . . . . I know, you want to warn him don't you? But you know the rules; and good ole prince Nathan has to play by the rules." Morrow chuckled hard as he spoke.

Mr. Sloan lay at the very end of the alley behind a bunch of boxes breathing hard, and trying desperately to hush his loud labored breathing. He looked around himself trying to find a weapon of some sort. He saw a two by four board, and pulled it in close to him-though he knew he hadn't a chance.

Snow kept easing patiently . . . . step by step . . . . inch by inch; Slowly looking behind each over turned item or trash . . . . step by step . . . . ease one foot down, then ease another foot down, guns glaring . . . . Step by step . . . . Inch by inch.

Streaks of sweat slowly ran down Mr. Sloan's face and splashed hard upon the cool pavement and mingled among the already soiled trash that he lay upon. His palms sweat, and his heart raced like a galloping horse about to finish his race.

Suddenly, sirens filled the air, coming closer and closer. Snow knew that cops would be upon him in a minute. The sobering thought uncomfortably eased upon him that Mr. Sloan would escape tonight.

"Damn." Snow whispered to himself, now easing backwards out of the alley. He didn't realize it, but he was only a few feet from Mr. Sloan's hiding place, but he'd rather approach him right and not make any mistakes than rush him and perhaps also die in the process.

He turned out of the alley, put his guns under his coat, and ran down the street to his car. As Snow hurriedly crossed the street, the chief of police stood on the side walk talking to one of his officers. He noticed Snow crossing the street. Their eyes locked for a moment. He discreetly nodded his head at Snow-motioning for him to leave the seen; for seeing Snow, the chief already knew that Snow, no doubt, had something to do with these shootings; but he was on Snow's pay roll, Snow stood by the car as the policemen's cruisers rushed pass him to the car wreck and the men lying on the ground, a few bleeding and a few dead.

Snow watched as Mr. Sloan eased out of the alley and walked towards the policemen with a big smile on his face. He looked across the street at Snow, smiled, hunched his shoulders and yelled at Snow, "We'll finish this later."

"Count on it." Snow hissed to himself.

Mr. Sloan, looking all ragged and dirty, threaded his way through the crowd, going to his car. While approaching his car, he looked back through the crowd, between the bobbing heads and shifting shoulders, and saw Snow still standing beside his car glaring hard at him.

"Wait a minute," said Mr. Sloan to himself, stopping in his tracks in mid stride. "Why he ain't left with all these cops around? Why he still watching me? Wanting to see me get in my car."

Mr. Sloan turned around, and walked over to the sidewalk across the street in front of his waiting Mercedes.

"Excuse me young man; would you go get something out of my car for me?" The twelve year old street kid looked at Mr. Sloan like he had cursed him. "Ok, I'll give you twenty bucks."

"Twenty bucks just to walk across the street and get something for you out that Mercedes," said the young lad. "Ok, it's your money."

"My briefcase is on the back seat; reach in and get it and bring it to me. I've got to talk to this gentleman here." Mr. Sloan turned to an unknown man and pretended to talk to him while watching the young boy, out the corner of his eyes, walk to the car.

"Easiest twenty bucks I ever made." The young boy whispered to himself as he reached for the door handle of the car. He opened it, and looked onto the back seat-no briefcase. "Crazy old man." He whispered.

He stood back up and looked back over at Mr. Sloan. "Ain't no briefcase in here." He yelled.

"Ok." Mr. Sloan yelled back, and took a step off of the sidewalk, heading for his car. He looked down the street, and saw Snow rushing towards them yelling something that he couldn't quite understand. "No second chance today dog." Mr. Sloan whispered under his breath.

The young boy, in frustration, slammed the door shut.

BOOMMMMMM!!!!!

A bomb sounded, and shot pieces of metal from the car everywhere. The force from the bomb slung the twelve year old boy across the street and slammed him dead into a brick wall. The crowd hit the ground screaming-as some of them were also hit by flying metal.

Mr. Sloan rose to his feet, and walked over to the young boy lying chard and dead on the sidewalk. "Nawl son, that was the hardest twenty dollars you ever had to make." He reached down and pried open the young boy's hand, and took the balled up twenty dollar bill from his smoking hand. "Figured Snow might of booby trapped it with a bomb." He looked down the street at Snow, still standing in the middle of the street and glaring angrily at him

Mr. Sloan tilted his head at Snow, smiled broadly, and then disappeared into the crowd as policemen waited for the ambulance and the coroner.

"Well, I must be going Nathan. Shall we say that it's been a blast hanging with you a lil while," said Morrow sarcastically as he snickered under his breath. "You know um always busy, and my work is never done," He waved at Nathan and disappeared amidst the shadows.

Nathan didn't reply, he just walked towards the crowd, hoping that he could help the fallen men in some way-as sorrow eased upon his face for the young boy-an innocent victim of a wicked old man.

CHAPTER SIXTEEN

Lorna and V walked casually out of Chang chow, an upscale Chinese restaurant where dignitaries and everybody that was somebody frequented.

"Girl, thanks so much for lunch. I been wanting to go there, if but to sit at the table and drink some water, but never could find a niggar to take me," said V smiling.

"No problem girlfriend; it's time for us to live a little."

"I heard that." V said as she high five Lorna.

"Let's roll on over to the Hood; I want to show you a piece of property that I got my eyes own. I want to open up a community center for the neighborhood."

"You go girl. I ain't mad at you."

They got in Lorna's Mercedes, top down, and cruised the long way back across the tracks to the Hood on Martin Luther King Drive. They sat, with the wind blowing in their hair, looking like two voluptuous African queens. Lorna was dark with smooth skin and full round lips; lips that most women would die to have-those full kissable lips that make grown men become boys and blush. V was just the opposite of Lorna; she was light skinned; her Mama was white, and her daddy was a jet black Nigerian. She had big grey eyes, and small lips; and smooth accentuated cheekbones that sat atop dimples that punctuated V's million dollar smile; both their bodies were very curvy, more than most women—The kind of curves that most women would die to have, and most men would die to call his own.

Al Green rang out loudly from her CD player, singing Love and Happiness. People on the sidewalks stopped what they were doing and took notice of the beautiful sisters cruising by in the black Mercedes, top down, and Al Green blasting.

"Now that's what um talking bout," yelled one of the sisters on the sidewalk to another.

"Yea, girlfriend represent!!" A tall slim sister sang out to passing Lorna and V.

Lorna and V just smiled and threw up their hands to them in appreciation as they cruised on.

"Why can't I meet one of them, or a sister like them?" A young ball head fellow sitting on the curve said to one of his fellows standing by.

"Cause you broke as hell," snapped one of his friends amidst laughter. "Women like that don't deal with broke niggars."

"Look, I ain't no broke niggar," he said, pulling out about forty dollars worth of cash from his pocket.

"Niggar that ain't no money; that won't even take a woman like that to dinner."

"Her ass better super size it at McDonalds." They all burst out laughing.

"That's why um a get rich, or die trying, cause um a have me a lady on my arms like that." One of them said, watching Lorna and V Mercedes disappear down the street.

"That's right son; is you gone dream, dream big," said an old man sitting on a garbage can playing chess with one of his friends. "Shoot, when you get our age, it don't even matter no more."

"Well, I ain't never fixing to get that old-where I don't want to kick it with a nice looking sister."

"Son, time has a way of catching up with you," said the old man still looking down at the chess board meditating upon his next move.

"That's why they make Viagro," said the young man laughing hard. "Man, I'd be popping them babies like M and Ms."

They all burst out laughing; even the old men playing chess had to stop and laugh.

Lorna and V eased to a stop in front of a large old boarded up store connected to a line of other small stores-most empty. A group of men and women stood on the corner talking, and a lot of them passed by going here and there.

"This is it girlfriend," shouted Lorna as she pointed to the building.

"Looks like a lot of work to me," said V, staring at the empty building over her sun glasses that now rested upon her nose.

"I know, but we're going to have fun fixing it up."

"We? What? You speaking French or is that just the side effect of that big Chinese lunch we just had?" V whipped, now staring at Lorna.

"Now you know you my girl, and we're going to do this together."

"When were you going to let me know?"

"Um letting you know now," said Lorna laughing.

They got out of the car and walked up to the front door of the building. V looked down a few doors and wondered what the crowd was for.

"What's going on down there," said V.

"Don't know and don't care," snapped Lorna.

"Girl, you fixing to move into the area; you better get to know the people and know what's going on." V said, pulling Lorna along side her as she strode closer to the crowd.

A man was standing on top a table talking to the listening crowd.

"Who is that?" V whispered to one of the ladies that were listening so intently.

"Ssshhhh" She put her finger over her lips to V. "It's Jamaal; the brotha is deep-makes you think." She whispered to V without taking her eyes off of Jamaal.

"See, what's wrong with most of us is that our bodies been set free, but in our minds, we're still slaves; that's why we act the way that we do, and the reason why we treat each other the way that we do. The other day, I heard some mixed up brothers saying that we can no longer blame the white man for our ploys cause ain't no white folks in our community; but my brothers and sisters I beg to differ with the confused brother. No, he doesn't live in our neighborhood, but you can bet your last dollar that he is still in here. The drugs in our neighborhood, he sends them. Don't none of our folks own air planes, or ships-no, the white man does that and gives it to his flunky to distribute to us; so we break into each other's houses, and rob each other, and kill one another for that stuff that he sends into our community." Jamaal rang out excitedly, filled with anger, as his deep set dark eyes peered sharply out over the listening crowd. "We make up less than twelve percent of the nations population, and yet we make up more than 70 percent of the prison population. Something is wrong with that picture alone. We're supposed to be the minority in jail also according to the percentage, but those flunkies think that is just the way it turns out. They even got our crazy butts mixed up in church too. Negroes pimping us in these so called churches!!

He driving a Bently, a Mercedes, or some expensive car, and living in a fine house while he tells you to take your rent money and your bill money and give it to him, while he shouts over the TV that God's gone bless you for that. You get thrown out of your house; your lights get cut off, and you losing weight cause your monkey crazy butt can't afford food cause you done gave your last to the church pimp. I don't believe that the God I serve is pleased with that. You on your knees praying 'lord bless me with my rent money', and he's saying back to you, 'I already did-you just gave it away'. He blessed you to pay your bills; and because you keep giving that pimp your bill money, you keep struggling . . . . A mess."

"That's right brother; that's right." A woman sang out.

V and Lorna were astonished at how intently the crowd listened to Jamaal.

"But the bible says for us to tithe," shouted one of the men angrily.

"Yea, it does; But, that's in the Old Testament Bro. Jesus is in the New Testament where you are, and Jesus doesn't even mentions tithing. He mentions giving-sometimes that means that you will give more than the Old testament tithe. But, God doesn't want you not to pay your bills so that you can tithe. The church pimp does cause that's how he gets to drive his fine car, live in his fine house, and wear his fine clothes-from your bill money. Now watch this, when you need his help cause you about to be put out, or your lights are about to be turned off, or you are out of groceries, he ain't fixing to help you. He tells you that the church don't do that, or his pimping butt ignores you altogether. He won't even loan you the money, which is your money. He tells you that the church does not make loans . . . . Wake up! The New Testament says that you should owe no man nothing; in other words, pay your bills. But, you avoid the bill collector, knowing that you owe him, so that you can pay your tithe. You robbing your creditor to put in the church . . . . Think for a moment-would God want you to rob somebody to give to him?"

"My ass don't even go to church, so he ain't talking to me." Lorna whispered to V.

"Me either, but um a start cause girl I ain't fixing to go to hell. I ain't fixing to live in hell and then die and go to hell." Lorna whispered back.

"Ssshhhh," another woman gestured, looking over at them. "He's going to take questions in a minute."

"Look, get yourselves together. Ain't nobody going to love you more that you love yourself. You expecting the president to stop the drive bys in our community. Didn't you see the news the other day; he can't stop the drive bys at the White House, so how's he going to stop them in our community? We got to do that! Love yourself, and be happy with you and your pretty black skin cause ain't nobody better at being you than you." Jamaal blew everybody a kiss as he jumped down off the table shaking hands as he walked.

The lady standing along side V and Lorna motioned to Jamaal to come to her. He walked up to them, shaking hands and talking briefly to others as he went.

"Brother Jamaal, these two sisters have some questions for you," said the lady pointing at Lorna and V.

"No . . . . No . . . No . . . We don't have any questions." Lorna and V said simultaneously.

Jamaal just smiled as he stuck his hand out to shake V's. Nervously, V stuck her hand out. "And how have I missed such a lovely flower in my community?" Jamaal said, holding V's hand firmly. "You are like a ray of sunshine on a cold dark night. My pleasure to meet you . . . . My name is Jamaal, and what's yours?"

"My name's Valery, but everybody call me V."

"Why?"

"Why what?" V asked looking sternly at him.

"Why they call you V when Valery is such a pretty name."

V blushed while Jamaal still held onto her hand firmly.

"Ah kumm." Lorna cleared her throat trying to let V know that she was still there standing beside her.

"Oh . . . . Oh . . . . Oh, excuse me, this is my best friend Princess . . . . Er . . . I mean Lorna." V stumble, still got her eyes on Jamaal.

Jamaal looked at Lorna, and smiled broadly and said, "Beauty always begat beauty. If you want to see something beautiful, just follow something beautiful."

Lorna blushed, flashing that pretty smile for all to see.

"Look, Valery and Lorna, would you all do me the honor and have lunch with me. I am famished, and I hate eating alone," said Jamaal pulling them along as though they had already agreed to go. "So what are you all doing here?"

"We're about to open a community center in the old building a few doors down." V said beaming as she spoke.

Lorna just smiled cause she knew that V was in with her business venture for good now.

"Get out of here!!" Jamaal said excitedly, stopping in his tracks. "Thank God, that's what we need here. That will help get some of them off the streets. I knew you were an angel."

Just then, an old woman screamed out, "Stop . . . . Stop . . . . Stop . . . . Please, somebody stop that bastard." She struggled to run after the fast running young man.

"Excuse me ladies," said Jamaal as he swiftly trotted off across the street. He tackled the young man onto the ground. "Where you going so fast lil brother?"

"Who . . . . Who . . . . Who the hell are you? Captain save a hoe?" The young man shouted at Jamaal while flaying his hands trying to punch Jamaal in the face to get him off of him. "Get off me man . . . . Get off me . . . . I ain't going back to no jail.'

"Hold on bro. Ain't nobody fixing to send you back to jail. Hold on," said Jamaal, trying to calm him down. "But you got to give mama her purse back."

Lorna and V crossed the street to get a better look at what was going on. "Girl, I don't know should we be mixed up in this?" Lorna said between breaths as they trotted across.

"I told you girl; we got to get in the know cause we're about to be business owners here," shouted V back at Lorna as they moved in closer to Jamaal and the struggling young man.

"Oh yea . . . . Oh yea . . . . Skuse me baby." The old lady said to V as she lightly pushed her aside. "Just hold him baby and let me wear his young ass out."

"Now hold on mama," said Jamaal, trying to restrain the young man with one hand, and restrain the old lady with the other. "Will somebody help me here?"

The old lady kept trying to hit the young boy with her umbrella. "Hold him still baby while I whup his ass," though she hit Jamaal most of the time, the young man lay there still struggling to get up while holding his hands over his head.

Laughing, V lightly grabbed the old lady, and guided her a few feet away.

"Nawl, don't hold me baby; don't hold me. Um a whup his young ass."

Most of the gathering crowd was laughing. "That's right, whip his ass Madea." A young lady yelled out. "They always snatching somebody's purse or breaking in something."

"Don't worry baby; grandma got this." The old lady said, trying to get away from V.

Jamaal helped the young boy up off of the ground. Again, he tried to run off, but Jamaal held onto him firmly. He grabbed the old lady's purse and handed it to V to hand to the old lady.

"Wasn't nothing in it anyway," said the young boy, now calming down and ceasing to struggle.

"I tell you what; everything better still be in here," said the old lady as she opened her purse; "don't um a whup your ass some more."

Jamaal motioned his head at V for her to take the old lady down the street away from the young man.

"I think that he means for you to help mama move on away from here." Lorna leaned over and whispered into V's ear.

"Oh . . . Oh . . . My bag." V said smiling.

"You ain't from round here is you baby?" The old woman said as they walked away. "I whupped his ass didn't I?" She said proudly.

"Yes mam you did," said V.

"If you don't want to go back to jail, why you keep doing the things to get you back in jail," said Jamaal.

The young boy dropped his head. "I don't know. Ain't nobody trying to hire me cause I ain't finished school . . . . so I hustle."

"Yea, hustle your way back to jail-huh? Become a career criminal."

"Yea, it is what it is dude."

"Mama you have a good day here." V yelled out. The old lady just threw up her hand and walked on mumbling to herself-waving her umbrella in the air.

"Now what you gone do?" Jamaal asked the young boy.

"Just hang out like I always do."

"Tell you what, you're going to work with me for now on. Ok."

"How much you paying?"

"Does it matter, it's more than you're making now ain't it."

"Yea, I guess so." The young boy answered looking down.

V and Lorna walked back up to Jamaal and the young boy. "We are about to go." V said, hoping that he would insist that they still had lunch with him.

"Oh no, y'all promised to have lunch with me. You can't go back on your word can you." Jamaal looked into V's eyes as he spoke. "I got to show you around our Hood don't I."

They began walking to the other side of the road. The young boy turned to walk in the other direction. Jamaal grabbed him by the arm.

"Aren't you having lunch with us?" Jamaal asked. "You work with me now."

"Nawl, I got something to do?"

"What?"

"Snatch another purse," snapped Lorna sarcastically under her breath.

They all stopped and looked at Lorna smiling.

"What?" Lorna asked.

"We heard that remark," said V.

"I don't care. Um use to being talked about," said the young man.

"I am sorry," said Lorna. "I was just joking."

"So we all going to Miss Bernice place for lunch-right?" Jamaal commanded.

"Ok." V and Lorna churned in.

"Ok . . . Ok . . . . We double dating huh." The young man said eyeing Lorna up and down.

"Not in your wildest dream bro." Lorna whipped rolling her neck.

"Well, Miss Bernice makes some collard greens that a make you want to slap your mama; and those candied yams, Lord have mercy. Y'all are going to love this community. Come on, I'll introduce you all to everyone on our way."

They turned the corner and headed for Miss Bernice little restaurant. V hoped that she wasn't dreaming feeling the chemistry between her and Jamaal. Lorna just walked and listened while Jamaal introduced them to one person after another. The young man walked closely to Lorna trying to pretend to onlookers that she was with him. He just kept looking at Lorna and smiling.

"You a nuff to make a niggar go straight." The young man whisper softly to Lorna.

"Please, ain't nothing you can do for me." Lorna said looking at him with discuss.

"Don't let this age and this size fool you." He smiled, peering over at V and Jamaal as he spoke.

Jamaal just shook his head and smiled. V kind of smirked. The young boy just kept grinning and looking at Lorna.

CHAPTER SEVENTEEN

Willie and Quitta sat in a booth at Bobo's place and sipped on a couple glasses of wine conversing about the last few amazingly wonderful weeks that had just past in her life.

"Quitta, all um saying is that everything that shines ain't gold, and Mama always said that if it seems to good to be true, then it usually is," said Willie.

"I know that Willie, but your Mama ain't never had nobody to do all of this for her over night . . . . We ain't had sex or nothing."

"Yea right; you don't know what he did while you was knocked out." Willie snapped.

"Trust me, a woman knows."

"Well, I hope that you are happy. I done got back in the church. I guess I'll find me a church girl."

"Done got back in? When were you ever a church goer?" Quitta said with a big smile.

"Now you didn't even have to go there. Cause your whole family are heathens, don't mean that everybody else is," said Willie jokingly. "Really, God's been too good to me for me to be acting like I been acting. If I put him first, everything else will fall into place."

"Well, um a get back in . . . . er . . . . start going to church too." Quitta stuttered.

Just then an argument started at the bar-two men yelling and pushing each other.

"There it goes," said Quitta. "Niggars always got to be fighting about anything, everything, and nothing. And you wonder why I want to get out of here . . . . Please."

"Ok . . . Ok . . . . skuse me." Willie got up and walked over to the bar to talk to the two men that were arguing.

"Hey brothers; what's the problem? Can I help?" Willie chimed in on the intense arguing.

"No!" One of the men yelled at Willie.

"Yea, who died and left you in charge of us." The other man whipped at Willie looking at him angrily.

"You best be going on back over there in the corner with your hoe." One of the men said as he poked Willie in the chest with his finger. The other man got up from his bar stool and walked towards Willie also-now, not arguing with each other, but ready to jump on Willie.

"Damn, niggar gone get his self killed," said Quitta as she jumped up from the table and rushed over to Willie and the two men. "Come on Willie, let's get outta here." She pulled Willie by the arm towards the door.

"Better be glad your hoe came to save you." One of them shouted after Willie.

"Who you calling a hoe? I don't see your Mama here nowhere." Quitta said, turning lose Willie's arm and walking back towards the two men. She got up in one of their faces-close enough to kiss.

"You gone let that hoe disrespect you like that dawg?" The other man said to the man that Quitta stood in his face.

Without warning, streaks of pain burst and zoomed across Quitta's face as her body slammed to the floor after absorbing a sweeping hard slap across the face. Stunned and crying, she struggled to get up. Tears flowing hard down her face, she looked for her purse that was flung across the floor as she fell. She wanted, needed her purse, for she always carried a switch blade in it . . . . And now, she felt she needed to slice some meat as she had done so many times before.

Willie ran over to her. "Quitta, you alright?" Willie said, helping her off the floor.

"Just give me a second; I got this. I bet his ass won't slap another woman when I get through with him." She was still looking around the room for her purse as she spoke while tears continued to stream down her face.

"Ought to know a woman's place." The man who had slapped Quitta said proudly as he looked over at his friend for confirmation.

"That's what um talking bout!"

Willie leaped upon both of them-hollering as he swung his fist at them. He was not much of a fighter, but he had had all that he could take this night. Quitta, the woman that he loved, had been insulted and bruised; he had to do something.

Willie, a big man, fell on one of them and started punching wildly. The other man fell hard into the bar, and grabbed his side amidst a torrent of pain. Blood trickled from his nose.

"That niggar done broke my nose." The man shouted to anyone that was listening.

Unsurprisingly, Morrow, in his black suit as usual, sat at the end of the bar in a darken corner smiling softly as he peered over at the broken nose man bleeding and leaning on the bar. He sipped slowly from his glass of Vodka straight, no ice. Still glaring at the man, Morrow reached into his breast pocket and pulled out a long hunter's knife, and slid it down the bar to the pain riddled man.

"Thanks bro," said the man as he grabbed the knife.

"My pleasure," said Morrow, tipping his glass to the man as he spoke and grinned. "Always want to help."

Willie jumped up, grabbed Quitta, and ran for the door. The man with the knife took chase.

A leg extended, covered in white linen pants, tripped up the chasing man with the knife. He fell and rolled onto the knife; slicing through his chest like it was butter, the knife severed his aorta-killing him instantly.

"Should tell your people not to play with knives." Nathan said coolly, gazing over at Morrow.

"Damn, should have known it was you! You ever mind your own business?" Morrow whipped at Nathan.

"Do you?"

"But you just killed him. Isn't that against the code or something?" Morrow said rising up from the bar, and taking his last big gulp of his Vodka.

"I didn't kill him. I just tripped him; besides, it was his time. He just chose how he was going to go; surely, you hadn't forgotten that Morrow?"

Willie, holding Quitta by the hand burst out of the club. Two policemen stood a few feet from the door with guns drown pointing at Willie and Quitta.

"Oh Lord Quitta!" Willie shouted looking down the barrels of the policemen's guns.

"Put your hands up and turn around!" One of the policemen shouted at them.

"Yes sur," said Willie throwing his hands in the air and turning around as fast as he could.

"But we ain't done nothing," shouted Quitta. "It's the men inside."

"Just turn around," said the policeman, gun still pointing at Quitta.

"Just turn around Quitta . . . . Just turn around . . . . Please!!"

They were handcuffed and put in the car.

"Girl, I ain't never been so glad to get in a police car in my life." Willie said to Quitta while he stared at the policemen as they slowly, with guns drawn, entered into the club.

"Why you care so much about a piece of dirt?" Morrow sneered. "Nothing but a hunk of dirt. Why you always trying to save them all?"

"Not trying to save them all," said Nathan, "just a few, the ones that's been assigned to me. You've forgotten how it works? You've forgotten what you use to do?"

"Use to is the key word brother. I woke up. Can't be stupid forever."

"Woke up-huh, more like kicked out is what you meant to say isn't it?" Nathan spoke softly, calmly, as a prince talking to his subject.

"Win some, lose some."

"Stakes are high aren't they?"

"Yea, but that's what makes it most interesting. Everybody ain't going to heaven prince Nathan . . . . You know that. I just assist them in making their decision. Why you always got to be up in my business? My people are always talking of your interference."

"They are all merely ignorant children that have lost their way," said Nathan.

"No, they choose to go astray, I just give them reason to stay."

"But some of them have great callings on their life, a calling that they don't understand; like Willie for instance. You see the anointing on him. I am here to assist him-wake him up."

"Calling? Huh, it's just a piece of dirt with a seed in it."

"Yea, that I am suppose to help fertilize and grow."

"Well, hark," Morrow playfully put his hand to his ear. "Duty calls. I'd like to chat longer dear prince, but as you know, I am about business-got to go and try to defertilize a piece of dirt." Morrow chuckled as he walked off into the shadows of the bar.

Nathan shook his head and walked outside and smiled after seeing Willie and Quitta sitting in the back seat of the police car.

After awhile, the policemen walked back outside, leaned into the car and said, "Who killed the man on the floor inside?"

"Killed who?" Quitta said, eyes widened.

"Lord Jesus . . . . Oh Lord Jesus, I didn't mean to kill nobody."

"So you killed him?" The officer asked Willie.

"Oh Lord Jesus help us cuzz you know we ain't meant to kill nobody." Willie closed his eyes tightly and prayed out loud.

"What made you stab him?"

"Lord help us in this hour of . . . ."

"Willie will you shut up and listen! We ain't stabbed nobody." Quitta shouted at Willie as she slapped him hard side the head trying to get him to listen.

"Stabbed? Oh no sir, I was too busy running . . . . er . . . I mean trying to get my girl out of there. I ain't stabbed no one."

"We didn't even know anybody was stabbed; we were too busy running away from the man," said Quitta.

CHAPTER EIGHTEEN

"Is this the house?" Aunt Louise asked as their car pulled up into the yard of a white and black house whose yard was meticulously manicured.

"I don't know," said Big Ma. "Leroy go knock on the door."

"This looks like some white folks house." Uncle Leroy said, easing the car door open.

"Just go knock on the door Leroy. Um tired," said Aunt Louise, wiping her brow.

"Ok . . . . Ok . . . . Ok . . . ."

Uncle Leroy walked up to the front door and knocked hard-too hard. He was nervous and anxious, and hadn't had his usual drinks to calm him down. Big Ma and Aunt Louise sat in the car and waited patiently. They had driven eight hours to see their nephew's in-laws. It had been almost six months, but they still grieved over Johnny, for he was their hope of at least one of them coming out of their small community and making something different of himself. They lived in a small town in south Florida where everybody worked at the Sugarcane plant. They made a decent living working at the Sugarcane plant, no a good living, so very few grew up and moved out; the world outside of the Sugarcane town was just that-the world outside. Everybody knew everybody in their town, and going out of town for them meant going to the nearest big city to shop and eat, and be back home before sundown; but Johnny was different-everybody knew it. When he was growing up, he was one of the few youths that didn't like the Sugarcane business, and was determined to go to college and do something else.

Though they oftentimes complained about Johnny, secretly, he was their hope, their dream because all of them imagined leaving their small town and seeing the world, but was too scared to venture out-so they saw the world through Johnny. They were so proud when Johnny moved to New York; though he was homeless most of the time before meeting his wife, Julia, still, he was their home town family hero for making it out of Sugarcane town.

"Who is it?" A lady's voice sang out from the other side of the door.

"Er . . . . Mr. Leroy." Leroy yelled back nervously.

"Mr? Lord have mercy." Big ma smirked aloud.

Uncle Leroy motioned his hands for her to hush. He could hear the chains on the door clanging as the woman attempted to unlock the door. Finally, Miss Eleanor opened the door.

"Why hello," said Miss Eleanor.

"Hey," belted Uncle Leroy, just standing there with a big grin spread across his face.

"Oh yea, you are one of Johnny's family members. I remember you from the funeral."

"Yea."

"Come in . . . . come on in." Miss Eleanor stepped back and motioned for him to come in.

Uncle Leroy started to walk into the house.

"Leroy!!" Big Ma snapped, trying to be loud and proper at the same time.

"Oh . . . . er . . . . wait a minute, let me go get my wife and mother-in-law out the car please."

"Sure," said Miss Eleanor with a big smile. "Joseph, we've got company."

Old Joe and Mr. Ire was down stairs watching T.V. "Who is it?" Old Joe yelled back.

"Surprise, come and see dear."

"Wonder who that is?" Old Joe said to Mr. Ire as they began to climb the stairs.

"I don't know, but um fixing to find out," replied Mr. Ire.

Uncle Leroy, Big Ma, and Aunt Louise stood in the Living room talking to Miss Eleanor when Old Joe and Mr. Ire walked in.

"Hey! Come on, have a seat," said Old Joe, motioning for them to sit down. "Man, its good to see y'all."

They all sat down in the Living room and began reminiscing about all the ones that they had lost in the bomb. Miss Eleanor cried and laughed at the same time. It was as though, for a moment, Julia and her family had come back to see her. Old Joe just laughed so hard when he spoke of past times with T.C and Poochie; and, of course, Mr. Ire remembered the many tight situations that Doctor Pee Wee and his nurse had gotten him and Snow out of.

"Have y'all heard from Snow?" Uncle Leroy said a little apprehensively, for it was as though all of them tried hard to avoid mentioning Snow for fear of upsetting Miss Eleanor.

"No, we haven't," said Miss Eleanor, dropping her head to hide the obvious hurt.

Big Ma swung her purse at Uncle Leroy, brushing him on the shoulder. "If you had a brain, we'd be rich."

"What? What I do?"

"Oh, it's alright. I've put my grand son in the hands of the Lord; only he can fix this situation. Frank Junior is filled with hate and revenge, and nobody can help him now but God. He's carried a lot of hurt and pain every since the day he watched his father kill his mama."

"Lord knows Miss Elli you carry around a lot of pain," said Big Ma; "you got to turn it over to Jesus, and stop worrying about it. He a fix things. He knows where your grandson is and he's watching over him because of you."

"Thanks. I never did catch your name."

"Everybody back home calls me Big Mary, and my children calls me Big Ma."

"Ok Miss Mary," said Miss Eleanor.

"Big Mary!" Uncle Leroy exclaimed loudly.

Big Ma just turned and rolled her eyes at him.

"Well, um just saying that's what they call her affectionately of course." Uncle Leroy said, trying to explain. "Big Mary, Big Ma, both full of love."

"Leroy, if I was you, I'd stop while I still got all my teeth."

They all burst out laughing. Uncle Leroy shuffled in his seat and smiled. He loved Big Ma; he just liked arguing with her and aunt Louise his wife.

"You all want something to eat or drink? I can fix you something if you like. I just bought groceries."

"Yea, I am a lil hungry," said Big Ma.

"You always a lil hungry." Uncle Leroy whispered under his breath.

Aunt Louise smiled at him, and whispered, "You better be glad she didn't hear you."

"Tell you what, let's cook a big dinner to celebrate our coming together as a new family," said Big Ma, getting up from her chair and grabbing her purse. "Let's go to the store. Do y'all have a market round here?"

"But I just bought groceries," said Miss Eleanor.

"I know, and I don't mean no harm, but I know how white folks eat. We need some collared greens, some chitterlings, some ribs, some fried chicken, some good ole mack and cheese, and maybe a peach cobbler to top it all off."

"Now that's what um talking about," shouted Uncle Leroy. "Gentlemen, where is the man cave in this establishment."

Old Joe and Mr Ire laughed softly, and pointed down stairs.

"What y'all got to drink down there?"

"What you want? We got Scotch, Bourbon, Vodka, Gin, Hennessey, and a few cans of beer if that's what you like." Old Joe said proudly as they began to go down stairs.

"Lord ham mercy, I done died and gone to heaven," said Uncle Leroy.

"Louise don't let me forget to get some fat back, hog malls, neck bones, and some pig tails for seasoning . . . . Lord knows food got to taste good."

"Ok Big Ma."

"I guess I am in for a treat-huh," said Miss Eleanor.

"Yes you is baby." Big Ma said as she excitedly exited the door with Miss Eleanor and Aunt Louise following close behind her.

"If you got any friends, you can invite them over cause she always cook like she is cooking for an army."

"Ooh," said Miss Eleanor with a big smile.

CHAPTER NINETEEN

It was Wednesday night, and Snow sat at home in his uptown apartment cleaning his two pistols. Lorna sat beside him and watched as she sipped on a glass of wine. He looked hard down one barrel, then the other, and ran a small brush saturated with gun oil down both barrels.

"I like watching you do your thing," said Lorna.

"These babies have kept me through thick and thin; they've sent a lot of folks to hell." He spoke softly without ever taking his eyes off of his guns.

"Sure hope you love me as much as I can tell you love those guns. I . . . ."

Quickly, Snow put his finger to his lips, signaling for Lorna to be quiet for a moment.

"What?" She kept talking.

Snap . . . . pop . . . . bump . . . . click . . . . In a moment, before Lorna could utter another word, Snow had his two nine millimeters back together with a full clip in both and one bullet resting in the chamber.

"What?" Lorna said with alarm as she nervously placed her glass of wine down on the table.

Snow leaned into her, still watching the front door, and whispered, "Keep talking loudly."

"About what?" Lorna said, now whispering.

"No, don't whisper. Talk loud about anything, everything, just keep talking." Snow whispered as he pulled Lorna behind the couch, and pointed both of his pearl handled guns at the front door.

Lorna just started talking about everything; she was now scared and nervous. Her heart raced like a thousand galloping horses in her chest.

Suddenly a soft gentle squeak of the floor in the hall on the other side of the door eased into the room and rested upon Snow's trained ears. He eased the hammer back on his pistols, and slid to an adjacent wall.

Lorna just kept on talking as if deep in conversation with Snow, and every now and then Snow would say uh huh, or something to make whoever it was on the other side of the door think that he too was deep into the conversation. Streaks of sweat ran down the side of Lorna's face; her palms sweat, but she kept talking. She motioned to Snow with her hands held out and empty, motioning that she had no weapon, but needed one. Snow pointed to the end table behind her. She kept talking loudly as she reached over, pulled opened the end table's drawer, and there, in the drawer, was the biggest gun Lorna had ever seen in her life. It was a 357 magnum. She was startled; she looked over at Snow and whispered loudly, "Are you serious?"

. . . . Another soft squeak from the other side of the door; now right in front of the door.

Lorna quickly grabbed the heavy gun out of the drawer and eased back close behind the couch. Snow motioned for her to keep talking. She started back rambling, with Snow's occasional uh huh.

Suddenly, they could see the door knob slowly turning back and forth. Lorna talked faster and louder; she could hardly breathe. She reached over and grabbed her glass of wine and took a big gulp from the glass, wiped her lips on her sleeve and pointed the big 357 magnum towards the door; come hell or death, she was going to fight with her man, or die with him.

CHAPTER TWENTY

"Lord Jesus, I ain't never been so glad to get in a police car in my life, and then be just as glad to get out of it too," said Willie as he looked deep into Quitta's angry eyes.

"Scared? Hell, um mad," said Quitta. "Did you see that dog slap me on my face? Did you see that Willie? If he wasn't dead, I was going to kill him the first chance that I got."

"Well, thank God that it is over."

"I wish Snow had been here." She said, rubbing her face.

"for what?" Willie snapped. "So he could have slapped him too."

"Now you don't even believe that one do you?" She whipped back.

"See, if he was here, me and Snow could have whipped them together."

"Yea right," said Quitta amidst a soft chuckle. "Boy stop."

"You just don't have no faith in me do you?"

"It is what it is Willie." She said shuffling in her seat. "I need a drink."

"I'll get you another glass of tea."

"Willie I need something stronger than tea."

"Remember the last time you drank; you woke up and didn't know where you were . . . . with that Snow character." Willie argued.

"And . . ."

"Lord ham mercy, there's just no hope for you girl; you let a pretty car and a lil money buy you out."

"Please!!"

"You know we could have been killed by those men Quitta?"

"For real though, thanks for coming to my rescue. You jumped both of them for me. You could have been hurt Willie."

"I was girl. You didn't see how hard he slapped me while I was on top of him."

"How you gone let a niggar slap you when you on top of him?"

They both just burst out laughing, and enjoying each other's company as none other could; and though Quitta would never readily admit it, Willie made her feel better than anybody else could. He just didn't have anything-no money, no car, no house; and she didn't want to wait until he got them. She loved Willie, but would never tell him or anyone else. It was her secret. She needed things and stuff; things that she knew, right now, Willie couldn't give them to her; so she settled, so she thought, for Snow-a big time street gangster.

They sat and talked at their little hole in the wall restaurant for hours, and drank Bud lite beer that they bought from the store next door; they laughed, argued, agreed, and even got mad at each other a few times, but they hung out all night-even after their boss had closed the restaurant and locked the doors.

"Y'all lock the door behind you when you leave," said their manager as he walked out the door and disappeared down the darkened sidewalk.

"Ok Mr. Franks, we will." Willie yelled out.

"Who you yelling to? He gone." Quitta slurred; "and what we locking up for? Nobody wants this junk."

"Now Quitta, you know niggars round here will steal anything that's not tied down. Have you forgotten how many times that they done broke in this place."

"Oh . . . . Yea, you right."

"I think that we're drunk Q," said Willie, and then took a big gulp from his can.

"You ain't had but two beers all night, and I been chugging them down like water."

"Still, um feeling no pain."

"You can't drink."

"I don't want to drink; I like being in control. What if something happen while we're drunk?" Willie said struggling to stand up.

"We'll run like hell together." She snickered. "No, for real Willie, What we gone do with our lives? We can't just work in this hole in the wall forever. God just has to have a bigger plan for our lives . . . . don't he?"

"Why people always want to talk about God after they get drunk?"

"Cause alcohol helps you get over your inhibitions and talk real stuff. But, my grandmother always said that God has a plan for all of us. Is it his plan for us to be struggling sometimes like we do-always looking at what everybody else got and we ain't got a pot to piss in."

"Sometimes Quitta, it is a part of God's plan; struggles gives us strength, and teaches us patients, and how to wait on God," said Willie soberly.

"God, I get so tired of where I am. Truth be told Willie, I really don't want to date no gangster, but what choices do I have?"

"You always have a choice Q; that's why you need to go to church and be around other believers."

"I want to go to church. I just don't like church folks. They are soooo judgmental and hypocrites. I hear them down at the beauty salon talking about their pastor and each other. You know if they talk about each other, they sure gone talk about me." Quitta spoke with her face resting in her hands.

"Your relationship is between you and God, not the folks. We go to church to hear the Word and get strength from other believers. Being saved don't mean that you are perfect; it means that you've given your life to Christ and that you're trying to live your life like him. Christians are not perfect. We're always struggling with something. It is a growing process. So yes, sometimes we talk about folk, and sometimes we argue, and sometimes we might even cuss here and there, but we are still saved; it just means that God is still working on us." Willie looked deeply into Quitta's eyes and spoke with passion and truth.

"I know but"

"No, there are no buts; you've got to choose the Lord for yourself; it's about your walk with him. Cause if truth be told Quitta, God is all you got, but he is all you need." Willie preached. "You think that white boy Snow would be into you if you didn't have no pretty face and nice body?"

"Oh, you think I gots a nice body?" Quitta asked with a big smile.

Willie blushed and smiled, and then dropped his head like a little boy. He shuffled his feet, and looked back up at Quitta.

"Well yea, you've got an awesome body, and some banging hips . . . . Oh God I got to stay focused." Willie raised his hands in the air in a prayerful gesture. "I don't have all the answers, but I take life one day at a time, and ask the Lord to use me. Some folks would say that I was wrong for jumping on those men, but God understands because he knows that I was trying to save a friend."

"Oh look Willie, the sun is coming up," said Quitta pointing out the window. "We'd better leave before Mr. Franks comes back and want to put us to work." Quitta staggered to her feet as she spoke, pointing at the window.

"Yea it is; good you live right around the corner cause we ain't driving," said Willie. "I'll walk you home."

They eased out of the hole in the wall restaurant and talked and walked playfully towards Quitta's apartment. Dawn was creeping down the streets while a few early birds were beginning to venture out for one thing or another.

Quitta reached into her purse and pulled out her key and dropped it into Willie's hand. Willie opened the door and motioned for Quitta to go on in.

"I'll see you tomorrow; well, later today sometimes," said Willie. "Now go on in and lock the door before I leave."

"Ain't you going in first to make sure my house is empty and safe." She giggled. "You still my hero aren't you?"

A big smile eased across Willie's face as he stepped into Quitta's apartment. He leaped from room to room playing like he was Superman or somebody as Quitta followed behind laughing hard.

"Ok, all safe."

She threw her arms around Willie's neck and squeezed him tightly. "You know I care about you more than anybody," she said, lips almost touching Willie's. "No, I love you Willie; really I do."

"Whatttttt!!"

Willie could no longer resist, he pressed his moistened lips softly against her waiting wanting lips. Quitta whimpered and held Willie even tighter. She wanted to pull away; wanted to scream for him to stop; wanted desperately to not like this kiss, but she did . . . . Oh god, how much she liked and needed Willie's kiss right now. She needed his touch; needed to feel his breaths upon her neck, needed to feel his big masculine arms around her waist.

Her lips locked in his, kissing a kiss that seemed like eternity had stopped for them, and eased them into that place that God had designed just for lovers. Slowly, she tried to pull away; Willie still holding her, still kissing, not wanting it to ever end.

She tore her lips away; her body still pressed hard against his. She tried to move away, but he refused to let her go.

"Willie please . . . . oh please . . . . Dear god please!"

He could not speak; just moaned softly in her ear, and hoped that he wasn't dreaming.

Quitta looked back into his deep brown eyes of care filled with passion. "But . . . . But . . . . But Willie it won't work . . . . It won't . . . ." She whispered softly amidst deep labored breaths. "Willie it won't . . ."

Amidst her sentence, she leaned forth and kissed Willie again, hard and deeply; her body now yielding completely to Willie's every movement. She was in love with Willie, and her heart was not about to allow her brain to interfere. He didn't have anything to offer her but his heart, and right now, that was all she needed-a man that loved her for her.

CHAPTER TWENTY ONE

Slowly V pulled her car up to the Community Center. Workers were busy trying to put it all together for her and Lorna. She got out of the car with her painted on jeans, and a pull over jersey tied in a knot in the back—exposing her tattoo at the lower part of her back. She strolled slowly up to the building looking all around at the building and the many workers trying to put it together.

"Hello Miss Valery," said one of the workers, putting down his tool and walking towards her. "Good to see you; we'll have this baby finished in a lil while."

"I just came to check on the progress. We're excited to move in and get things rolling."

V barely looked at the man as she spoke, though all the men in the building had stopped working and was gazing at her. She looked down the sidewalk hoping to see Jamaal somewhere. The sidewalk was filled with people, most just hanging out and talking, but no Jamaal.

"Look, y'all doing a great job. I got to go down a few doors and holla at a friend of mine." V said as she walked away-commanding attention with every practiced step. She knew that all eyes were on her, and as usual, she purposely gave them something to imagine!

"Now that's what um talking about-make a old man want to live again," said an old man with a saw in his hands.

"Stop old man; all a woman like that would do is kill you." One of the younger men said to the old man.

The other workers just laughed hard while the old man stood there grinning.

"Have any of y'all seen Jamaal?" V asked the young men sitting around talking.

"Lord ham mercy." The man exclaimed as he turned around and looked at V.

"Damn!" Another moaned.

"He down in Miss Bernice place." One of the men said, pointing down the sidewalk to Miss Bernice restaurant.

"Thanks," said V as she eased away walking like a model on a runway. She acted as though she didn't notice, but she knew that all of them was staring at her-well her jeans, but she loved the attention. She had practiced this walk for years; now it came easy-it was her walk.

Finally, she reached Miss Bernice restaurant. She stood at the door and peeped in and secretly listened to Jamaal as he spoke to about seven young men gathered around his table.

The young men sat and listened to Jamaal intently. "We've got to break this slave mentality that we've acquired over the years. We're free, but we still act like slaves. We still wait for somebody else to do for us that for which we should be doing for ourselves. I think that it was Booker T. Washington that said that the Negro buys what he wants, and begs for what he needs. We've got to stop waiting for someone else to make things better for us-wake up, we're not slaves no more." Jamaal said, motioning his hands in the air and looking sternly into the gazing eyes of the young men that savored his every word. "We walk around here driving a car with 22 inch realms and a blasting boom box, and all of it cost several thousand dollars to put on an old car that's worth only a few hundred dollars, and yet we won't take care of our own children. You driving a Cadillac, and parking in the governmental projects. Please! Brothers walking around here with gold chains around their necks and wearing designer shoes and name brand clothes, and yet, his babies got to depend on Welfare and food stamps to survive. It's the slave mentality; the slave had the baby, and Mr. Charlie took care of it-he expected Mr. Charlie to take care of it."

"Yea, the white man is still holding us back." One of the young men said with a hint of excitement mixed with apprehension.

"Nawl bro. Ain't nobody holding you back. Are they trying? Yes! But, ultimately you are in control. We go to school for free, but the dropout rate among us is still very high, and most of us don't even choose to go to college. We brake our backs for somebody else, and collectively, we make over a billion dollars a year, and yet the Indians, and Iranians, and Pakistanians, or some other foreigner will come into our community and open up a store and bleed all of our money out. We should have our own stores; our own schools, even our own banks, but we'll never have any of that as long as we continue to think and act like a slave."

"Gosh, this guy is so deep." V whispered to herself.

"Come on inside baby and sit down and listen; Jamaal is one of our young prophets," said a young lady as she pulled V into the restaurant with her. "Just sit down; I'll get you something to drink while you listen. Isn't he just wonderful?

V eased into a chair in the back of the restaurant, and listened intently to Jamaal as a spoke to the young men.

"We live in houses that we really can't afford; drive cars that we can't afford-you driving a car that you got to pay on every month for the next six or seven years of your life. Does that make any sense? By the time you pay your note on the big house that you had to have, and the high note on the latest car you had to have, and after you pay your other bills, you only have just enough for gas to make it to the next pay period-so you have no money in the bank and you live from pay check to pay check. See, now, ain't nobody making us a slave, we choosing to be a slave; matter of fact, we happy being a slave. The slave was a commodity; he fueled the economy. The free slave is still a commodity, and still fueling the economy cause as soon as we get paid for our labor, we happily take it and give it all back to Mr. Charlie, but it's not just us black folk; no, many white folks too have chosen to be slaves and live from pay check to pay check, and give any excess money back to their slave owners-the system."

"So, how do we change it Jamaal? Most of us are there. We are struggling, but I still got a pretty good credit score." said one of the young men.

"Credit score . . . .Hah." Jamaal laughed. "Brother, all a credit score does is tell the man that you have faithfully made the notes on the stuff that you got in the past that you could not afford; cause that's all a good credit score is-it let you get stuff on credit that you otherwise cannot afford. That's why most car dealers don't advertise how much the car cost; they just mention over and over again the small monthly payment; cause they know that the slave is only going to look at the low monthly payment. Remember, slavery is always about money."

Jamaal had noticed V in the back of the restaurant, but finished his conversation with the young men.

"Hopefully, I was some degree of help to y'all today. We got to stop thinking like a slave, and start thinking like free men that don't want to be a slave no more." Jamaal got up from his seat, and shook the young men hands as he made his way back to V.

V stood up, watching Jamaal start to walk towards her. She touched her chest and tried to calm herself. Her breaths were short and filled with excitement. A big pretty smile strode across her ruby red lips while her teeth glistened like bursts of sunshine. Nervously, she stuck her hand out to shake Jamaal's as he took the last few steps towards her.

"Hey . . . . Hey . . . ." She said like a little girl.

"Hey you," said Jamaal with a big smile as he gently took V's hand then bent over and kissed it like a prince would.

V blushed; her cheek bones turned red; being light skinned, it was often hard for her to hide her emotions.

"And what do I owe this wonderful pleasure to?"

"What . . . What?" V stuttered.

"Your presence of course; it is not often that a man gets to behold such beauty during his day. I am overwhelmed, to say the least." Jamaal flashed his gentle smile at V as he spoke. His masculine shoulders, broad and erect, stood like two mountains adorning his neck. His bald head, smooth and polished, beamed softly at V. His goatee, trimmed and tapered, accentuated his dark lips; his dark skin was smooth and velvety wrapped upon his muscular frame. She felt like a little girl meeting the school boy she secretly had a crush on.

"I . . . . I just came to check on the progress of the Community Center." She said nervously.

"Wow, don't you look amazing," said Jamaal as he took her hand and slowly swirled her around.

V smiled broadly and giggled a little as she turned around in front of Jamaal.

"Girl you are something; really something."

All the other men in the restaurant stared at V and Jamaal as they talked.

"She bad ain't she brothers?" Jamaal, still holding V's hand and turning to the men, asked with a big smile on his face.

"Oh god yes!" An older gentleman chimed from behind the counter.

They all laughed and shook hands, agreeing with the old man's sentiments.

"Yea, I gots to agree with pops." One of them said.

"Me too." Another one belted out.

"Ok . . . . Ok . . . . Ok, y'all can go back to doing what y'all were doing," said Jamaal playfully.

"This is what we were doing-looking at y'all." One of the young men said.

"Well, do something else." Jamaal said, playfully picking up a napkin off the table and throwing it at them. "Come on; I'd better get you outta here while I still can."

Jamaal held V by the hand as he guided her out of the restaurant.

"You always dress like that?" He said, as they stepped outside.

"Like what?" V said, putting her hands on her hips looking up at Jamaal with a big smile.

"Like this." Jamaal said motioning his hands down V's body.

"I just threw on a lil something."

"Yea, right." Jamaal whipped with a grin. "A lil something to drive men crazy.

"Is that a compliment?"

"Yea, but I wouldn't want my woman to dress like that."

"Ok, now um really concerned. You know you got to explain yourself mister." She asked still smiling.

"I just believe that some things a woman has should be for her significant man's eyes only."

"What?" V asked.

"Those sculptured hips of yours should be for your man's eyes only; and that sexy tattoo down your back, I thought the tattoo was for your man, but if you showing it to everybody, then it's for everybody," said Jamaal. "I mean, I ain't trying to judge you, but you asked; and I guess um being a little presumptuous, but if you were my woman . . . . Well."

"Well what?" V asked still smiling, almost glowing from Jamaal's suggestion of them being a couple.

"Let's just change the subject . . . . Just know that I think that you look absolutely great."

"Thanks," said V. "Ok, now how did you become so deep?"

"What do you mean?" Jamaal asked peering over at V as they slowly walked down the sidewalk. "You know um just the invisible man walking on the side of you; don't you?"

"Why you say that," she asked.

"Cause you know all eyes are on you and those banging hips of yours."

Again she blushed and playfully pushed Jamaal on the shoulder. "For real, how did you get so deep?"

"Well, life taught me; through struggling, and troubles, and debt, and when I went to jail, it allowed me to think."

"So, you've done some time?"

"Yea, at the time, it was the best thing to happen to me; it opened my eyes, and made me not want to be a slave no more," said Jamaal, looking over at the rising sun just beyond the buildings. "Why? You have a problem with that?"

"No, I respect you a lot. I don't meet many brothers like you."

"Is that a compliment?" Jamaal asked smiling.

"definitely, you're different."

"You see, most black folks are blind and mixed up. They going around here celebrating Emancipation Proclamation."

"Why what's wrong with that?"

"Well, Abraham Lincoln's Emancipation Proclamation was not something that he just decided out of the goodness of his heart. It was a strategy of war. It said that all the slaves in the states in the South that was fighting the Union were free. It didn't include those slaves everywhere else-they were still slaves."

"Wow, didn't know that one."

"And, freedom, well, all the other nations were abolishing slavery. The U.S and Britain were among the last that followed suit; and slavery was no longer as profitable as it was cause cotton in the south were on the decline-it started costing more to have a slave."

"I like that." V said softly. "An intelligent man . . . . Well, good looks don't hurt none either."

They both just laughed out loud as they walked on. V felt better than she had ever felt about a man in her life. For the first time in a long time, she could imagine herself changing and becoming a wife, a mom . . . . Oh god, she couldn't believe that she was actually thinking that, but it was secretly what she had always wanted.

The day eased into night, and they found themselves, after a couple of hot dogs, sitting on a bench in the park listening to the crickets while they nestled together and watched the glistening moon.

CHAPTER TWENTY TWO

Snow leaned against the wall, still pointing his pistols at the front door; Lorna just kept rambling on. Snow wasn't saying anything now, he just stared at the front door with his dreads laying softly upon his shoulders.

The floor softly creaked again.

"Ain't this a trip. Those dipstick dumb monkeys out there don't even have sense enough to sneak up on somebody," sneered Morrow. "Dumb dirt."

"Did you really think that they were going to surprise Snow?" Nathan said with a smile. "I mean come on Morrow."

"Well, it ain't quite over yet. Sometimes even a stupid piece of dirt can do something right."

Suddenly, the front door burst opened; masked men ran in with guns drown, and shooting as they came.

Snow squeezed his triggers, spitting bullets and sending one masked man to hell after another.

Lorna pointed her gun, closed her eyes, and pulled the trigger. The 357 roared and spit a fiery bullet across the room at the unwanted intruders. The gun kicked Lorna back under the table. Lorna's bullet hit one of the masked men and slammed him against the wall like a ragged doll.

"Good lord." Lorna yelled as she scrambled to get from under the table.

One after another, over and over, they kept coming in, blasting aimlessly; but, Snow kept sending them to hell as they came.

Again, Lorna propped back up behind the sofa, aimed, and fired another shot, and again the 357 slammed her back up under the table; This time she shot through the wall, hitting the man even before he got to the door.

Finally, the mask men stopped coming. Snow could hear footsteps slamming to the floor as one of the surviving mask men ran down the hall. Ten men lay upon the floor dead.

"Well, I'll just be . . . ." Morrow said shaking his head in discussed. "How you shoot that many times, and hit no one; not even his bimbo wife."

"You on the wrong side Morrow. You don't expect to win do you?" Nathan said, looking down at the men lying on the floor dead.

"You had something to do with this." Morrow screamed in anger.

"No I didn't. Now you know that, unlike some folks, I follow the rules . . . . We can only observe until commissioned."

"There be other times Nathan . . . . Other times . . . . You can count on it."

"Now that, too, I am sure of."

Smoke eased out of Snow's two nine millimeter pistols and disappeared towards the ceiling.

"You alright babe," said Snow, leaning against the wall with pistols still aiming at the front door.

"Yea, um alright," said Lorna. "How you shoot this thing? It's a cannon . . . . Gosh, it's a wonder that you can hit anything with it."

"You put down two of them."

"For real."

"The one over there, and one outside in the hall."

"Outside in the hall?" Lorna exclaimed bewildered. "How I do that?"

"That cannon goes through sheetrock like its paper."

Suddenly they heard sirens blasting in the air coming towards them.

"Po po coming." She said nervously.

"Yea, I hear them."

"What should I do? Let's get outta here."

"No, just put your gun on the table and let's move to the other side of the room and do whatever they tell you to," said Snow as he laid his two pearl handled pistols on the table.

Lorna nervously flung her gun onto the table like it was hot. "Now, what we gone tell them Snow?"

"Tell them the truth. You don't have to prop up truth. We heard somebody coming; we got ready for them; they burst through the door and we shot them dead as they came first shooting at us. That's the truth. Don't tell them nothing else, and don't volunteer information about anything-tell them what they ask for."

"Ok, got you." She said, then flopped onto the couch beside Snow who had crossed his legs and sat back comfortably on the couch as he waited for nearing sirens with cops to arrive.

CHAPTER TWENTY THREE

Aunt Louise, Uncle Leroy, Big Ma, Old Joe, Miss Eleanor, and Mr. Ire sat on the second pew in the church-Saint John Baptist church. The choir sang spirited songs, as members sang along, some shouting out loudly hallelujah and amen. Big Ma raised her hands and sang along.

"What time this over?" Uncle Leroy leaned over and whispered in Aunt Louise ear.

"Just enjoy the service Leroy." Aunt Louise whispered back.

"Um trying, but this suit is too lil and these new shoes you bought me is too tight; how um spose to go to sleep in here this uncomfortable."

"Lord ham mercy; you ain't suppose to go to sleep."

"Will y'all shut the hell up; we in church, have some respect." Big Ma leaned over, putting a fan to her mouth and whispered loudly, snapping as she spoke.

"See there, your mama is going straight to hell; cussing in church," said Uncle Leroy rolling his eyes at Aunt Louise.

"She ain't cussing; hell is in the bible."

One of the ushers walked up to their pew and cleared his throw very loudly-giving them the hint to be quiet.

"What?" Uncle Leroy exclaimed, looking up at the usher.

The usher simply put his finger to his lips.

"It's her," Uncle Leroy whispered loudly back at the usher as he pointed to Aunt Louise.

Miss Eleanor, Old Joe and Mr. Ire just sat down there and smiled during all the commotion.

"Boy, ain't they a lively group," whispered old Joe into Mr. Ire's ear.

"Crazy is a better word." Mr. Ire whispered back.

"Can we change seats?" Uncle Leroy whispered into Miss. Eleanor's ear.

"What?"

"Just slide over and let me sit there by Old Joe and you sit here."

Miss. Eleanor nodded her head as she slid over, and Uncle Leroy sat next to Old Joe.

Suddenly, everybody stood to their feet, clapping and shouting loudly as the pastor walked onto the pulpit.

"What's going on?" Uncle Leroy asked, standing to his feet.

"The pastor just came in."

"I thought it was Jesus, way these folks hollering up in here." Uncle Leroy mused.

"Praise the Lord saints," shouted the pastor, a very short fat man with a tapered beard and bald head.

"Praise the Lord!" The whole church shouted back, clapping loudly again while some shouted hallelujah as loud as they could.

The pastor preached about an hour on how good it is to be saved. Uncle Leroy slept most of the service. Aunt Louise hunched Uncle Leroy in the side to wake him up to hear the pastor's closing remarks on being saved.

"What?" Uncle Leroy said, looking at Aunt Louise bewildered.

She just pointed at the pulpit and said, "Listen."

"What? I been listening. You thank cause um sleep I can't hear?"

"You know church, unlike a lot of things, salvation is free. All you got to do is just say that you accept the Lord Jesus Christ as your savior, and you shall be saved. Jesus says to come as you are. If you are a liar, come on; if you are a thief, come on; if you are on drugs, come on; even if you are an alcoholic with the smell of booze still on your breath, come on."

Big Ma leaned over, looked down at Uncle Leroy, and made a sneering face as she gestured towards the pulpit.

"What? You know I don't drink. Um already saved." Uncle Leroy whispered loudly.

Old Joe dropped his head and giggled softly at Uncle Leroy, his shoulders bouncing up and down as he laughed. Mr. Ire joined the silent laughter.

Big Ma just shook her head at Uncle Leroy.

"The Lord is not looking for perfect people; he just wants somebody that he can use to show the world him; for it is not his will that any should parish and go to hell; he gives everyone the opportunity to be saved, and salvation is free." The pastor spoke sternly into the microphone as sweat eased down his brow and dropped upon his already wet coat. "You see, we're not perfect; we're all still growing in Christ. God is still working on us. There should be a sign stuck on our heads that says Under Construction."

"Your sign should just say Stupid." Big Ma whispered loudly to Uncle Leroy, smiling broadly as she spoke.

"You better be glad we in church Big Mary." Uncle Leroy whispered back.

The congregation started getting up and going up to the pastor and dropping money at his feet as he spoke.

"I need to be a preacher." Uncle Leroy said, leaning into Old Joe's ear.

Again, Old Joe just dropped his head and giggled softly.

"Leroy!" Aunt Louise whispered loudly, punching Uncle Leroy hard on his leg as she spoke.

"What?" Uncle Leroy snapped back. "Don't you want me to get some religion in me . . . . Oh, I can't be no preacher-huh."

"I didn't say that." Aunt Louise whisper, holding a fan up to her lips as she spoke softly to Uncle Leroy. "He used a jackass once, so surely he can choose to use another jackass."

"What? You talking bout me? Well, I don't see no wangs on your back."

"Sssshhhhhh," said a member in front of them, turning around with her finger to her lips.

"You sssshhhhh yourself," whipped Uncle Leroy back at the woman.

"Leroy!" Big Ma roared above a whisper.

"What? Why do everybody keep calling my name?"

"Lord ham mercy on this fool." Big Ma whispered a prayer to herself, and then leaned over and whispered into Aunt Louise ear. "Um a slap his ass right here in church if he keeps on."

"Mama!" Louise exclaimed in surprise. "You can't say that in church."

"Skuse me baby, but that niggar a make Saint Peter cuss."

"You know what, I ain't got to sit here in these too lil shoes and take all this abuse from y'all." Uncle Leroy got up to leave as he spoke. "Skuse me Old Joe."

"Yes . . . . Yes . . . . Yes, brother come on up to the front and testify to the church, for he already knows your heart." The pastor yelled at Uncle Leroy, trying to make his way out of the pew. "Come on brother share your heart with your brothers and sisters."

Uncle Leroy looked behind him, thinking surely that the pastor was talking to someone behind him, but no one was standing up but him. He looked at the pastor and touched his chest and mumbled, "Who me?"

"Yes, you brother. The Lord showed me that you going through something."

"Lord ham mercy." Big Ma whispered to herself as she frowned hard at Uncle Leroy.

Uncle Leroy looked down at Aunt Louise; she simply smiled at him and motioned for him to go on. Old Joe and Mr. Ire just sat there and giggled softly.

"Yes, come on brother," said the pastor again to Uncle Leroy.

Uncle Leroy made his way up and stood by the pastor and faced the congregation.

"The Lord showed me that you been going through a lot lately," said the pastor.

Big Ma and Aunt Louise knew that Uncle Leroy could fake a cry when ever he wanted, so when he burst out crying up front, they knew that he was putting on.

"Well I'll be damn," said Big Ma a little louder than she intended.

"Ma, her said a bad word," said a lil toddler sitting in front of them and staring at Big Ma while tapping his mother on the shoulder.

Aunt Louise just smiled at the lil toddler's words.

"He better turn around and mind his own business fore I spank his lil ass right here in church."

"Big Ma!" Aunt Louise exclaimed.

"Well," said Big Ma, "Children need to stay in their place; you know I don't play with children."

"Testify brother, gone and tell the saints all about it," said the pastor.

Uncle Leroy stayed up there for more than thirty minutes, crying and lying. After he had finished, the pastor took up an offering and gave it to Uncle Leroy to help him get through his troubles.

"Boy you going straight to hell." Big Ma said to Uncle Leroy as he passed by acting like he was crying.

Amidst his fake tears, he leaned over and winked his eye at Big Ma. She reached out and grabbed him. Aunt Louise grabbed Big Ma to pull her away from Uncle Leroy.

"Yes . . . Yes . . . . go ahead and let it out sister. Shout for the Lord," shouted the pastor to Big Ma.

Big Ma stopped, turned Uncle Leroy lose, and stared up at the pastor like a scared deer caught at night in headlights. She froze; her heart raced. Suddenly, she threw her arms into the air yelling and shouting.

"Yea, that's it sista, let him use you," said one of the ladies to Big Ma from the front pew.

"Lord ham mercy, all of us going to hell," whispered Aunt Louise, looking at Big Ma putting on, and glancing at Uncle Leroy exiting the front door with his offering in his hand.

CHAPTER TWENTY FOUR

Snow sat amid the still silence in his apartment; the police were now gone, and the coroner had removed all the dead men. His apartment was riddled with holes and burst out walls, and overturned tables, but he sat there in the still silence and pondered how and why God had allowed him to survive so many attacks by so many enemies; why he had survived being shot last year and be at the brink of death, yet not die; how he had stood up in a haze of bullets, and not even get a scratch.

He remembered hearing his grandmother's words echoing in his ear, "The Lord has a plan for you."

"Maybe God does." He whispered to himself as his eyes filled with tears.

Truth be told, he was tired of this life, the life that he had chosen for himself, but he had to pay one more debt before he got out-a debt he knew might very well cost him his life, but still, he had to avenge his sister.

From a little boy his life had been filled with violence, so violence came easy for him-it was a way of life. As a little boy, he watched his mother be strangled to death by his father, and watched as the police car took his father away forever. He remembered his grandmother coming and telling him and his sister that their father had been executed in prison. His sister, Julia, cried hard, but he refused to cry; by that time he was hard.

"Oh God, I want to yield and walk in your plan and will for my life, but I just can't right now . . . . I just can't." Tears rolled easily down his cheeks. "Lord if you will just allow me some time to avenge my sister, I will give you my life completely. I'll do whatever you want me to do, and go wherever you want me to go. I jus can't leave now with this . . . . after what that dog of a man, Sloan, did to my family."

"Look, ain't that pathetic." Morrow sneered looking down on Snow. "A piece of dirt trying to bargain with the Almighty. Now he takes stupid to a whole new level."

"Oh, you should talk. I think that some of their older ones have a saying for you," said Nathan.

"What?"

"The pot calling the kettle black." Nathan smiled.

"Cute Nathan . . . cute."

"You know I just call them as I see them, and do what I am told."

"Yea, you always were a flunky," said Morrow. "Don't you get tired of always doing what you're told? Don't you want to come outside the lines every now and then?"

"Nope."

"You're pathetic too; that's why you care for that piece of dirt so much-you relate." Morrow hissed.

Snow sobbed hard, remembering the many sermons he had heard his father preached; and he missed his mother so deeply. She read him and his sister bible stories at night when they went to bed-not a day pasted that he didn't miss what his family use to be. Now, Frank Junior was no longer Snow the hard street gangster; he was now just the kid, Frank Junior, that missed his family more than words could express-The Frank Junior that carried a lot of pain, tears, and hurt inside-The Frank Junior that very much wanted to serve God, and follow in his father's footsteps, doing God's will; the Frank Junior that he kept hid deep inside of him-hidden from the evil streets that would eat him alive in a just a few days.

He prayed and prayed, and asked God for forgiveness for all of his sins-though he knew that he would soon be killing again.

"See." Morrow snapped, frowning at Snow.

"What?" Nathan calmly said, never taking his eyes off of Snow. "Is not that the most wonderful prayer you've heard-prayer filled with hurt, pain, sincerity, tears and truth going up to the Creator."

“If I had to choose, I think Jezebel did a lil better,” said Morrow, “course, that was just before she fell out the window and the dogs ate her flesh; but still.”

“Leave us now dark prince.” Nathan whipped, looking sternly at Morrow.

“As you wish . . . . Holla.” Morrow was gone as suddenly as he had come.

Snow was still sobbing, and trying desperately to wipe the streaming tears from his eyes.

“So when are you going to stop fighting and walk in your destiny?” Nathan asked Snow with cords of compassion.

Snow jumped to his feet, reaching in his back for his pistols, he swirled around to Nathan, barely able to see for the tears.

“Must you always point those things. You know they will never save you.”

“They’ve saved me so far.”

“No, they hadn’t. I have been the one that have kept you . . . . Well, Hope to be more exact,” said Nathan.

“Why are you always doing that?” Snow shouted with much aggravation. “You gone mess around and get shot.”

Nathan just smiled.

"No, I am for real. Why are you always sneaking up on me? And, how did you get in here . . . . Though, I don't think I want to know."

"I am always where ever you are. We've always been with you."

"We," said Snow, putting his pistols back in his belt. "Who is this we? Oh, you talking about the weirdo in the black suit all the time."

"No, that's Morrow; though he can be quite irritating sometimes, he is not always around."

Nathan, still looking and smiling at Snow, motioned his hands towards Snow as if presenting someone. Suddenly, there appeared, a woman-a young woman; very beautiful. She had long hair that hanged upon her waist, and a smile that held the brilliance of the sun. Her skin looked velvety smooth, and her continence glowed like a consuming fire. She had pretty brown eyes, filled with love and compassion.

"Hello Frank," she said softly, smoothly.

Snow fell back onto the couch, mouth gaping open. He couldn't believe his eyes. She was the same woman that played with him when he was a child; the same woman that stayed with him in his room, and softly sang him to sleep at night when he was sick.

"But . . . . But . . . But . . . ." Snow stuttered, overwhelmed with surprise and excitement. "You're . . . . You're Hope."

"Yes, Frank Junior, now you remember me." Hope said evenly.

"Yea, and what happened to your mom?" Snow said, hardly taking a breath. "She would come in my room and talk to me sometimes too."

"Oh, you must be talking about Love; she was assigned to your mother; she just checked on you from time to time when your mother was worried about you, but I was the one with you all the time, even from the first breaths you took entering this world."

"But, why?" Snow stumbled.

"You'll understand it all later Frank. Right now, you need to stop this mad plan of revenge you have. Revenge only destroys you. You're in great danger."

"it is out of my hands. I had quit, and was about to leave town. Sloan started this war all over again."

"We know, but trust me, Sloan's end is fastly approaching; you must not get caught up in Sloan's last acts," said Hope softly.

"I wish that I could just walk away now, but I can't Hope; I just can't, so if I shall die, then I must die."

"Now that's what um talking about; that boy has a lot of me in him." Morrow said with excitement in his voice.

"That's what I am afraid of . . . . and, I thought I told you to leave?" Nathan said sternly to Morrow.

"I just couldn't resist ease dropping. I just love this dirt."

"I'll not tell you to leave again Morrow."

"Ok . . . . Ok . . . . Ok . . . . Always so serious; just chill and enjoy the ploys of the stupid dirt," said Morrow leaving even as he spoke. "See you around Prince Nathan . . . . see you real soon."

"We plead with you Frank Junior; you must alter your plans," said Love as she walked across the room and sat beside Snow.

Hope followed her and sat on the other side of snow, and softly placed her hand upon Snow's shoulder. He remembered her touch. It was so soothing, so comforting. He looked into Hope's eyes, as tears streamed down his own. Love put her hand on his other shoulder, comforting him.

Snow wept so hard, so bitterly; all of his hurt and pain that he had carried down through the years surfaced from deep within his heart where he kept them hid. He fell into Hope's arms, and wept long and hard.

CHAPTER TWENTY FIVE

Bam . . . . Bam . . . . Bam!!!! The front door to V's apartment screamed out. Without a second thought, V's eyes popped open from a soothing sleep; she reached under her pillow, grabbed her 38 snub nosed pistol, pulled the hammer back, and rolled onto the floor, pointing the barrel at the front door.

Her efficiency apartment was in the heart of the Hood where all the action was every night; and V had made up her mind that if it came down to it, she would rather go to jail than hell.

Bam . . . . Bam . . . . Bam!! The door screamed again. V still didn't say anything. She hardly breathed, waiting to send a bullet sailing to the front door.

"V, you there?" Lorna loudly whispered in desperation. "Girl, please, please, please be here."

V recognized Lorna's voice, and eased the hammer back in place on her pistol. Quickly she ran to the door, pistol still in her hand, and opened the door to a crying Lorna.

Lorna leaped into her arms crying and shaking all over. V held her tightly, as a mother would her ailing daughter.

"What's wrong? What's wrong?" V whispered into Lorna's ear. "Girl, you shaking like a leaf on a tree. What's wrong?"

Lorna just held onto V and wept, as V eased the door shut and locked it with her free hand. She eased Lorna over to her pullout bed, and sat down.

"I just can't do it V." Lorna stammered amidst tears.

"Can't do what girl?"

"Snow's a gangster." Lorna said, sitting back and wiping her face.

"I mean duhhh," said V sarcastically.

"I knew that he was, but I didn't know to this extent."

"What happened?"

"Last night there was a shoot out at our apartment. Ten men kicked our door down and came in shooting." Lorna said, between labored breaths.

"What? Snow's alright?" V said, jumping to her feet.

"Yea, he's alright; we were ready for them, and shot them as they came into the house."

"So what's the problem? Y'all killed they ass." V sat back down next to Lorna on the bed.

"Yea, but Snow said that he is sure that it ain't over. Either he's going to kill Sloan first, or Sloan won't stop until he is dead; when I left, he was getting ready to go looking for Sloan."

"Look, you can stay here for as long as you like; until things cool off a bit. You know Snow's going to handle his business."

"Yea, and I am hoping not to be a widow by the time all this is over." Lorna put her face in her hands and began sobbing some more.

V just sat beside her and rubbed her softly on her back-sometimes, to comfort someone, you need not speak a word; just be there for them.

"Look, we need to do something to take your mind off of all of this stuff," said V. "I know, let's go over and check on the community center, and see what we can do."

"Yea, you right, that might ease my tension a little," said Lorna nervously, "but what if they're still looking for us?"

"Don't worry girlfriend, I got you . . . . Now let's go." V got up off of the bed and pulled Lorna up along side her. She grabbed her 38 revolver and tossed it in her purse.

"Well, if something happens, I guess I'll just jump behind you-huh."

"No, I told you, I got you girlfriend." V walked across the room, reached under the cushion of the couch, and pulled out a black 9 millimeter pistol. "This baby holds 15 bullets and one in the chamber."

"Why I got to carry the big gun?" Lorna said, walking over to V and grabbing the 9.

"Cause you carrying that big purse of yours; besides, with all of this power, we can shoot our way out of anything."

They slung their bags across their shoulders and walked out the door, eased into Lorna's Mercedes, and drove off-headed for the community center. Lorna knew full well that V also wanted an opportunity to see Jamaal again, but she was cool with that. She just needed to do something to get her mind off of what had happened the night before.

CHAPTER TWENTY SIX

"How the hell eleven men can't kill one man?" Sloan shouted at a group of men listening to his every word. "I did send eleven didn't I." He looked sternly at the lone failed assassin sitting in the midst of them scared and shaking.

"His . . . . His . . . . His girlfriend helped him; she was shooting too."

"Oh . . . . Ohhhhh . . . . That explains it; so it was eleven against two." Sloan said with an air of sarcasms as he walked towards the scared assassin sitting there sweating and now clearly shaking. He knew that Sloan would try to make an example of him so that the others would fear him. Live or die, he must at least try to strike first, no, he thought; he decided to just run at his first chance, then strike later. Sloan kept talking and slowly easing towards him . . . . "It's now, or never." He thought to himself. He jumped to his feet and dashed for the nearest window.

Mr. Sloan grabbed his gun, but before he could even point, the lone assassin shattered the bay window into a thousand pieces as his body sailed through; but he forgot, or didn't care that he was on the third floor. His body slammed to the hot simmering pavement below like a sack of tomatoes-splattering rich red blood everywhere.

Mr. Sloan and the others eased to the shattered window and looked down at the twisted bloodied body lying on the pavement as people gathered around him.

"Damn, what a waist," said Mr. Sloan.

"What?" Another of the men said.

"I just had that pavement pressure washed yesterday." Mr. Sloan uttered casually as he walked away from the window. "Can we get on with this meeting now?"

They returned to their chairs mumbling as they went-some visibly shaken by the incident, but Mr. Sloan was cool, calm, and collective as though nothing, or very little had happened. Though Mr. Sloan thought that he had sent a clear message of fear to all of them, it was just the opposite. His silent message to them was that he was crazy, and they'd better get him before he gets them; so all of them sat back down with a plan that they'll not end up like the man splattered on the pavement below.

"Gentlemen, the sooner we get rid of this Snow character, the sooner we can get back to business as usual." Sloan said as he lit a long cigar in his mouth then fumbled through a stack of papers.

They all knew that, even if they got rid of Snow-which none of them believed they would, it would never again be business as usual with Mr. Sloan at the head. Secretly, in their minds, they felt that they could live with Snow-just don't cross him; for Snow's fight was with Mr. Sloan; from that day on, mutiny was brewing and waiting for opportunity to come calling.

CHAPTER TWENTY SEVEN

"Child, didn't we have good service this morning?" Big Ma said excitedly to Aunt Louise.

"Yea, we did; and pastor brought a good message."

Uncle Leroy sat on the couch and counted his money from the offering while the others browsed through the house taking off their Sunday's best.

"You know you going to hell don't you," said Aunt Louise to Uncle Leroy.

"Yea, and your mama going to have an apartment right next to me down there."

"I sure wish that I could see my grandson right about now," said Miss Eleanor. "I miss him so much, and Lord knows I pray for him every day; that the Lord will keep him safe from hurt, harm, and danger."

"Why don't we just drive back up there and check on him?" Big Ma said, easing back into the room. "We can just rent us a big van and we all ride together."

"Yea, Leroy don't mind renting a van for us," said Aunt Louise looking over at Uncle Leroy as he stuffed his money into his pockets.

"Oh, y'all need Big Daddy now-huh." Uncle Leroy joked.

"Yea, we need Big Daddy now, or whatever you want to call yourself," said Big Ma. "Big fool is more like it." She whispered to herself.

"I don't know. It's such last minute," said Miss Eleanor; "and I don't know where we could find Frank Junior."

"That's why we got this street dog with us; he'll find him." Big Ma said, pointing at Uncle Leroy. "No offence this time Leroy."

"Oh, none taken. I'll find him if we go."

"Yea, let's go," said Old Joe.

"Um ready if y'all are. My clothes already packed, and I can't wait to see my boy Snow . . . . er . . . . Frank Junior," said Mr. Ire.

The next morning, they all packed into a long rented van and hit the road just as the sun was easing up over the distant grey mountains, and shooting light through the sleeping trees.

CHAPTER TWENTY EIGHT

It was early evening, the red sun nestled among the billowing radiant clouds, and threw streaks of fleeting light and sobering waves of heat upon an already warm crowd as they listened to Jamaal, standing on a table top as he spoke—The neighborhood profit; the rebel against organized religion; the hope for those tired of structured church without God, tickled their ears and intensified their desire for change and new relationship with the almighty God. He thundered words of encouragement and renewed joy to his small crowd of followers as drops of sweat raced down his face and leaped upon his chest, and disappeared, as the other drops did, upon his sweat filled shirt.

Like a city version of John The Baptist, Jamaal shot words of conviction and revised hope of truly getting to know an eternal God that organized religion had rid from the masses.

"They tell you to come to their church and get to know God, but I come to tell you that God is everywhere; on your jobs, in your kitchen, in your car, even in your secret place where you'd rather him not be." Jamaal chuckled a little, as did a few others from the crowd.

"Show you right brother," shouted a man from among the crowd.

"They tell you to come to their church, and I ask you why, and for what? For, every time I see them, they are fighting with each other, and the pastor, who they say that God sent him to them, and that he is the head of their church, they spend most of their time fighting with him. Don't tell me that there is peace in the valley when I see you just coming out of the valley with your nose bleeding, race tracks around your eyes, and your arm is broken. It's hard for me to believe. No! I don't want to go into that valley; I catch enough hell as it is."

The crowd laughed, while some shouted a vibrant amen with raised fist to Jamaal.

"How are you going to tell me that God sent you your pastor, when y'all spend most of your time fighting him. The Deacons, which suppose to be his helper, is his most adamant fighters. How you gone fight the man that you say God sent, or how you gone vote out of the church the man you say God has sent to you. It doesn't make sense to me. But, you say that he messed up is the reason why you vote him out; but I submit to you that he's just showing you that he is human-capable of mistakes and falling. They forget that forgiveness is the most powerful tool a child of God can use. You see, I don't need you to pray for me so much when um up and doing well; it is when I have faltered and fallen and can hardly get up by myself."

The crowd raved and high fived each other in agreement to Jamaal's piercing words of forgiveness.

"The reason why forgiveness is so powerful, is because it is a chosen act. You choose to forgive, even when the hurt and disappointment is still there. It is such a powerful act that God praises because you choose to forgive when you know that you can't forget." Jamaal thundered like a preacher Sunday morning from a pulpit. "Truth be told, all of us have got some stuff in our secret closets. I can't damn you because I got some skeletons in my own closet that um asking God to deliver me from. You see, the truth of the matter is, it takes everything we got to keep our own selves together. We don't have time to straighten nobody else out. God told us to just preach to them and lead them to him. It doesn't make my light shine any brighter if I put your light out . . . . No, we're supposed to shine together . . . . Amen somebody."

"This is so damned boring," said Morrow to one of his lieutenants standing next to him among the approaching street shadows. "Reminds me of some other loud talker with all that black and proud rubbish during the sixties. But, we'll soon see how much he believes that stuff. I see nothing wrong with those dead churches; people just go there to die; don't they."

"Yes dark Prince; you are right as always." The dark Lieutenant hissed, and stared angrily at Jamaal and his listening crowd.

Just then, Lorna and V eased up and stood in the back of the crowd and listened. A big smile of proud showed on V's face as she listened and fumbled with the gold chain around her neck.

"And our children in the community; our little black boys and little black girls, they are hurting; hurting to see successful black men and women in society; hurting to see happily married black moms and dads." Jamaal continued. "We can't blame it on nobody else now; it's us! If we continue, our little ones will have to go out and marry some white boy, or white girl to fulfill their dream. It shouldn't be! We've got to teach our young men to be men, and our young girls to be ladies, but it starts with us. You can't expect them to reach out, when all they see you do is settle. They'll only do what they see you do-period!"

"He is so good isn't he?" Lorna whispered to V.

"I don't know, but he sure looks like it."

"What?" Lorna turned to V startled.

"Oh, my bag, my mind was somewhere else," said V, slightly embarrassed.

"I'll say it was." Lorna said grinning.

"Ssssshhhhhh." One of the ladies said, motioning her fingers to her lips at them.

V just kind of rolled her eyes at her, smiled, and nodded her head in agreement.

"I know . . . . I know, um the only black man in the world that thinks desegregation hurt us as much as it helped us . . . . Why? Um glad that you asked." Jamaal went on speaking, flaying his arms in the air as he spoke. "Desegregation brought us better schooling, better housing, better jobs, and more opportunities, but it also taught our children how to be disrespectful to their parents; before desegregation, our children didn't talk back, or were disrespectful to us. No, they learned that from them—among other things. They learned to walk around with this entitlement attitude-like the world owes them something, so they work less and play more; expecting to be like the white man, but they fail to realize that the white man takes care of the white man, and they will never ever let you forget that you are black in a very white world. See, y'all think that Obama is going to save us. Obama can't save us, we've got to save us. You can't just sit back and say President Obama will save us. No, we've got to get rid of our "government will save us" mentality, and help ourselves. Even the churches now are asking the government for help. They call it 501C3 non profit status for the church, but they fail to realize that governmental help comes with strings. All they see is the money. Wake up people! Planned Parenthood cannot raise our children for us-we've got to do that ourselves. The national debt is increasing by trillions of dollars every year, and the whole world keeps pinching more from the U.S, and increasing our debt. Somewhere we're going to have to pay the piper! We've got to help us save us. We need to open our on stores. Folks come into our community and open up stores and take all the money out of our community, and you willingly take them your money-knowing full well that they care little about us."

Jamaal spoke for another thirty minutes, and then jumped down from the table pulpit, and shook hands and greeted his audience as he made his way back to waiting Lorna and V.

V started to primp her hair and adjust her blouse, hoping to look her best for the approaching prince. Lorna just looked at her and smiled.

"Girl, you got it bad." Lorna said to V, rubbing her on the shoulder.

"Is it that obvious?"

"Uh huh."

"Now that's what um talking bout." A young man's voice sang out behind Lorna.

She turned around, and caught the gazing eyes of the young purse snatcher she had help Jamaal with before, staring at her body up and down.

"That's what um talking bout right there. Couldn't stay away from me could you?" The young man said, rubbing his hands together, and smiling broadly at Lorna.

"Please, not in a million years. I don't do babies." Lorna whipped back at him.

His surrounding friends burst out laughing at him. "No . . . No, she just tripping cause of y'all," said the young man, trying desperately to salvage his little image. "She feeling me."

Jamaal walked up chuckling at the young man. He grabbed him around his neck, pulled him up close, and whispered in his ear. “Some things you already know you just cannot have.”

“Don’t know why his young ass always tripping,” said Lorna, and then moved to the other side of V away from the young man.

“Hey darling,” said Jamaal to V as he leaned forward and softly kissed her on the cheek.

V blushed and smiled. The young man followed Jamaal’s lead with Lorna. He walked around V and said to Lorna, “Hey darling,” as he leaned forward as if to try and kiss Lorna.

“Y’all better get this fool fore I shorten his days,” said Lorna, pushing the young man away with her hand covering his entire face.

“Let’s go get something to eat. Mrs. Bernice is still open, and um told that those ox tails are kicking today.” Jamaal said as he put his long arm around V’s neck and pulled her forward.

For the first time in over a day, Lorna felt a little at eased, and though she would never say it aloud, she kind of liked the attention the young man was giving her. She exhaled hard to herself as they walked towards Mrs. Bernice place; but still, with all of that, she could not shake the feeling that a storm was brewing and headed her way-a storm that she wasn’t rightly sure that she would survive.

CHAPTER TWENTY NINE

Snow cruised slowly down the streets in his 1965 Chevelet Impala; his 9s laying on the seat beside him, and his M16 laying on the back seat with a full clip and several other clips stacked on the floor. He even had a few grenades. He was ready for war, and he was looking for war. Somebody had to pay the piper tonight, and he hoped it was Sloan and his goons.

He turned down Blue Harion Boulevard; the Blue Harion Club had just begun to come alive. He heard somebody yell his name as he waited at the Red light.

"Snow . . . . Snow." A young man yelled out again.

Apprehensively, Snow pulled over, and eased to a stop. Usually, he wouldn't stop, but he needed information-where was Mr. Sloan.

Snow watched cautiously as the young man slowly approached his car. His 9s cocked and in his lap with his hands resting on the triggers.

"What's up?" Snow snapped coldly at the young man.

The young man reached into his pockets.

In a flash, Snow whipped up his 9 aimed at the young man, ready to send a bullet sailing, and send another man to hell.

"No . . . No . . . . No, hold up dog; I was just getting a cigarette." The young man said, shaking so until his cigarettes dropped and scattered on the pavement.

"Yea, what you want."

"Heard you looking for old man Sloan; well, I got some info on him that I thank you want to know." The young man nervously said.

"What?"

"Well, I ain't doing so well; and any other time I'd just tell you for free Snow, but um hurting right now."

"How you know I want put a bullet in you and make you tell me what you know?"

"I don't, but I shole god hopes you don't. I over heard some brothers talking in the bathroom; they thought I was drunk and passed out, so I just lay there on the commode and just listened to them talked."

"Well, what they say?"

"They said that they fixing to go somewhere in a lil while across town and shoot up your girl at some community center on the other side of town-the bad section called Cherry Hill."

"You sure?" Snow asked, rolling a couple of hundred dollar bills out of his pocket.

"Yea, um sure."

"Anything else?" Snow asked as he reached the two crisp one hundred dollar bills to the young man.

"No, but I'll keep my ears to the ground." He said as he grabbed the money and quickly stuffed it in his pocket. "Everybody calls me Skeet around here. You need anything, just ask for Skeet."

"Ok Skeet, if you hear anything else, hit me up on my cell; it's 555-1213. Call me anytime you even remotely think I want to hear something, and even when you don't think that it's important, call anyway. I'll make it worth your wile. 555-1213, remember it. You got it?" Snow asked hurriedly, easing off all at the same time.

"Yea, 555-1213; I got it." The young man yelled back at Snow as he squealed off in his Impala. He was glad and proud to have Snow's cell phone number, for he knew that he had something that a lot of people wanted, but few had-a way to get in touch with Snow when nobody else could.

Snow's black Impala zipped through the fastly approaching night like a bolt of lightening from a violent storm. He knew that he had to get there before the sun fully set; for that's when they would strike. Barely on two wheels he squealed around corner after corner, barely hitting his brakes. He hoped that he wouldn't pass any policemen on his way-for he couldn't stop; he wouldn't stop.

He just refused to loose another lady to a band of violence that he was caught up in. He had to save Lorna. He pushed the peddle to his Impala even harder-to the floor. It roared and screeched like death on a hungry path.

His tires hollered to a halt. Swiftly he got out of the car as darkness settled in. Snow slung the M16 across his shoulders, and tucked his 9s in his belt, and then reached into his glove compartment and grabbed another 9 and put it in his boot.

He raced towards the community center; Lorna's car was still parked out front.

Lorna, V, Jamaal, and the young purse snatcher were inside just having a casual conversation about how the Center would change Cherry Hill.

"Y'all got to take cover!" Snow yelled to them as he burst through the door.

"What?" Jamaal asked.

"Trust me, if he says for us to take cover, take cover and ask questions later," said Lorna as she pulled V behind a table, and pulled out the gun that V had given her earlier.

"You got any more heat man?" Jamaal yelled to Snow with his hands out stretched.

"Yea, here." Snow reached down into his boot, grabbed the 9 and tossed it to Jamaal.

V pulled out her snub nosed 38, and stared at the front door.

"Y'all got a radio or something in here?" Snow yelled out.

"Why?" The young man asked amidst confusion.

"If they don't hear any noise, they'll know something is wrong."

"On the counter over there by the flowers." Lorna streamed out.

Snow blasted the radio, then they waited for what seemed like eternity.

CHAPTER THIRTY

"Told y'all Leroy could find him." Exclaim Aunt Louise proudly.

"Yea, he can do something right-huh?" Big Ma said sarcastically.

"Y'all keep your eyes open over here. They say this Cherry Hill is something else," said Uncle Leroy as their rented van eased slowly down the street. "It's supposed to be a community center on this street somewhere."

They all stared out the windows of the van into the rough streets of Cherry Hill, hoping that they would find the community center before night fully set in. The streets were full of life-people going to and fro doing whatever their thing was. A few young men stood on the corner shooting crap on the sidewalk with obvious cans of beers in their hands.

Cherry Hill, with its dilapidated buildings and pot hole filled streets, and crime infested avenues, was still home to a great many people filled with hope and pride. If you were not from there, somehow instinctively the locals knew it; and looked at you like fresh meat in a hungry lion's den.

Eleanor felt uncomfortable, for she saw crowds of frowned black faces staring at her uncommon white face and ocean blue eyes, as if to wonder what was she doing there. She hadn't seen another white face yet; but to see her grand son, she had purposed that she would go through hell and high water, and obviously, God was holding her to her word-for Cherry Hill looked like hell.

Little girls were on the side walk jumping rope, while little boys were dancing to the beat of some thundering music. Lights in the various buildings started flicking on as night quietly moved into the busy streets.

"We'd better find this community center soon, or we gone have some problems." Uncle Leroy said, staring off into the crowd that stared back at him. "They don't look like they too happy to see us."

"Look," hollered Old Joe, "I think I see it. Is that it?"

"Pull up in front of it." Big Ma yelled.

They pulled up in front of the community center, and heard the music blasting inside.

"They show don't mind playing their music in Cherry Hill-huh," said Aunt Louise.

They all got out of the van. Miss. Eleanor's blood was running wild in her vain, and her stomach was queasy. She hadn't seen Frank Junior since the bombing that killed Julia and her family, but she wanted to see him, had to see him, if but for one last time.

CHAPTER THIRTY ONE

"What you gone tell Snow?" Willie asked Quitta as she sat across the table staring back at him.

"I'll tell him the truth; shoot, I ain't seen him since he gave me all those things. Guess um a have to give that stuff back-huh?"

"Yea, I think so; unless he don't want it," said Willie, reaching across the table and squeezing Quitta's hand in support. "You sure this is what you want to do?"

"I can't love but one man at a time; I ain't no hoe." She said. "My heart belongs to you Willie; as much as I tried desperately to fight my feeling for you, the truth is I love you-broke and all."

"Now see, you didn't even have to go there." Willie said with a big smile.

"I know, but every now and then, I have to pinch myself to make sure um not just a dreaming fool. You ain't got nothing and I ain't got nothing, and as Reverend Ike would say, nothing from nothing leaves nothing."

"But, we're going to have something together Q; you'll see."

Willie and Quitta sat in the dim light of a restaurant and talk over their decision to become an open couple. They were in love, had been in love, but denied it and fought it over and over again.

Sometimes it is as though Love has a warped sense of humor-putting some couples together that need not be-making East fall for West, knowing full well that they can never be together, but that's how love works sometimes. You don't always fall in love with the one that you need to love; no, your heart sometimes has a mind of its own, and loves who it wills. Our bodies just hopelessly yield to the strong desires of our hearts-even when our brain and other senses tell us otherwise. Love reaches deep down into the deepest darkest trenches of poverty and causes two people to fall in love, knowing full well that poverty is their plight, but love, in its unassuming splendor, gives the poverty stricken couple some degree of hope and happiness even in the midst of their sorrow.

Love makes a blind man see again; an old man young again, and a sick man feel well. No, it is not strange that love would bring two opposites together and cause them to forge ahead against all odds. Only love can make a broke man feel rich, and a lame man feel well; and love won't leave you during your lonely hours, and won't forsake you during your life's midnights-no, real love just refuse to let go, even when all seems dark and hopeless. Real love is the lantern that lights our paths and gives us roses sometimes during the bitter moments that life thrusts our way.

So, it is with this love that lingers upon Willie and Quitta that gives them the strength and psychological fortitude to go forth expecting that tomorrow shall be wonderful when life's forecast unveils horrible storms; that love that time, or place, nor distant space don't even matter, for they're all but grains of sand upon the seashores of time when it comes to love; they are but shifting pebbles resting upon the mountain side of life that true love finds away to connect.

"God's going to bless us cause he promised," said Willie.

"Promised who?" Quitta whipped. "I show ain't heard from him in a while. He ain't even been in my neighborhood in a while."

"Oh, he's been in your neighborhood, or else you wouldn't have no Hood. God has a plan for all of us. Sometimes we can't see it, and don't understand it, but what he allows us to go through is not in vain."

"You mean to tell me um going to be a preacher's wife-huh! Now Willie you know I ain't that strong. Why, I'd be cussing them deacons out, and cussing them nosy old sisters out. Boy, you better recognize God ain't through working on me yet, and um the first to admit that um a piece of work."

"He still working on all of us baby . . . . all of us," said Willie calmly, "and whether um going to be a preacher is all in his hands. I just want to be a vessel that he chooses to use."

"Well, anyway, um just saying up front."

"I know . . . . I know . . . . You keeping it real." Willie said with a big smile. "And, um sure God likes that."

Quitta sheepishly smiled back at Willie.

"Marry me Quitta?"

"Wha . . . . Wha . . . . What?" Quitta struggled, choking on a glass of wine after Willie's question. "What'd you say?"

"I said, will you marry me Q?"

"Lord ham mercy; that's what I thought you said. Willie, how we gone do that? Where we gone live? Shoot, how we gone live? Are we ready for this?"

"Whoa . . . . Whoa . . . . Just slow down; we'll take it one day at a time. I got enough saved up to get us a decent place."

"Where? In Cherry Hill."

Willie laughed hard. "Girl stop; I wouldn't put my enemy over there, so you know um not about to try and put my wife there."

Quitta took another big gulp of wine from her glass; looked at Willie hard again, then took the last gulp of wine from her glass.

"Let's go outside, I need some fresh air," she said, rising up from the table.

They rose up and walked hand in hand outside; Willie smiling all the way. Quitta didn't know what she was feeling, but it felt crazy, and scared, and wonderful, and exciting all at the same time.

"You know, to be a broke ass niggar, you sure know how to make a girl feel real good."

"You sure its not the Riesling wine." Willie said as they stepped out onto the sidewalk in front of the restaurant.

"Well, it might of helped just a lil bit." Quitta said amidst a hard giggle. "Gosh, these shoes have been killing me all day." She reached down and pulled her shoes off and stumbled into Willie in her attempt.

They both laughed hard and nestled into each other's arms. She stared hard into his eyes, and saw the place that she had long for all of her life-just didn't know that it had always been ever so close. She tenderly rubbed his broad shoulders, and then tip toed and put her arms around his neck and pulled him into her.

She kissed him, slowly and passionately as she dropped her shoes to the grown. The warmth of his lips upon her lips felt good and sweet to her; and feeling his cool breaths on her face during the kiss, soothed her and caused even her labored breaths to surrender unto him.

He wrapped his burly arms around her and pulled her into him even closer. They kissed for what seemed like forever. Their breaths became one; their hearts throbbed endlessly together as one. For the moment, it was as though God himself had ushered them into that place that he designed just for new lover-where new love thrives and never ends; where the past, the present, and the future collide and become one. He kissed her and kissed her like there was no tomorrow; that this kiss was the last kiss of all kisses-no doubt, better than the first kiss of Julius Caesar upon the lips of Cleopatra, and perhaps better than King Solomon's first kiss upon the lips of the very beautiful Queen of Sheba. A kiss that quivers, raises and unleashes even the very secret passions locked up deep inside your soul that's been hidden even from you-passions that perhaps are only equaled to that for which King David felt when he secretly peered over his balcony and beheld the bathing beauty of Lady Bathsheba.

Slowly, they pulled away; their lips easing apart. She stared into his eyes; her body limp and weak-now surrendered completely to its new owner. She was dizzy and could hardly catch her breaths. He stared back into her eyes, as only a king would his new queen. He leaned in to kiss her again, but she placed her index finger to his lips as she labored ever so hard with her breaths.

"We'd better stop while we're ahead; don't you gone have to be baptized all over again in the morning." Quitta said, slowly sliding her hand down Willie's chest, and gently pushing him away.

Willie just laughed hard and gazed at Quitta through his loving, caring eyes-eyes that now only saw her.

They walked slowly down the sidewalk; Quitta with her shoes in her hands-like they were in the world alone, and nothing else, or anyone else mattered.

"Hey, I got an idea sweetie," said Quitta.

"What?"

"Let's ride through Cherry Hill," she said.

"Now?"

"Yea, now."

"For what? You see it's getting dark out here? You do know that we don't want to be in Cherry Hill after dark-don't you?" Willie said, stopping and staring at Quitta.

"I know, but they're trying to change Cherry Hill. I heard that they have built a big new community center there. Let's go see it."

"You sure that's what you want to do? Cause you know um down. I ain't scared."

Quitta just started laughing hysterically, and trying hard to stop, but she couldn't.

"See, there you go tripping. Come on, let's go back to the car, and we're going to Cherry Hill this night . . . . Um a show you I ain't scared." Willie said, turning Quitta around and heading back to the car as Quitta continued laughing as hard as she could. "Lord help us." Willie said under his breath."

CHAPTER THIRTY TWO

Darkness was slowly swallowing the streets of Cherry Hill. A cool breeze leaped up over the old grey buildings and ushered a cool breeze down the streets of warm pavement that bottled the lazy heat and shot it upon those that walked by. An elderly lady stood preparing her home made podium, and her loud speakers and microphones. She stood on the corner of Martin Luther King Boulevard and Tenth street, with her huge Bible and religious tracks, and hollered at anyone that passed by her-far or near. The locals called her aunt Lilla. She was part of the weekend nights amusement for people that dared to come to the jumping night clubs and bars in Cherry Hill; like most poverty stricken neighborhoods, even though it was poor, it had its share of bars and night clubs that outsiders loved; maybe it was that tingling thrill of danger in the air, or maybe that fear of being held up and robbbed at any moment, but whatever it was, outsiders came to Cherry Hill every weekend by great numbers-packing into the night clubs and bars, and dance floors.

Aunt Lilla was there on the corner preaching every weekend come rain or shine. Sometimes her sister, Rose, would help her-though Rose was very shy. She was mostly there to watch over her hard big sister to keep her out of trouble because she knew all too well that if pushed, Aunt Lilla would physically fight with the best of them; so Rose just stood in the back ground and just handed out religious tracks to those that passed by while she monitored her big sister's actions. Aunt Lilla was a tall very large dark woman with white teeth that had one very shiny gold tooth that dominated her conversation when she spoke to anyone up close. She spoke with a deep Southern drawl from deep red lips. Her hair was long and curly and filled with grey locks that hanged to her shoulders. Her hands were large and filled with callous from working in the hard cotton fields in Georgia most of her early life. She was one of those that found Christ late in life, and just like most of us, Aunt Lilla had some unchristian like character that she just found it too hard to get rid of, or just when she thought that she had gotten rid of it, somebody would always force her to revert back-but, none the less, she remained trying to live a Christen life-though she used far too many curse words during her days.

Aunt Lilla screamed and shouted Bible verses, and old wives tales at anybody and everybody that would listen, and especially those passerby's that tried to ignore her, and the ones that she thought was surely on their way to hell.

"Y'all hellish scoundrels better come to the Lord while you have a chance." Aunt Lilla shouted to a few passing young ladies decorated in too much makeup and too tight short skirts. "Look at you, walking round here dressing like a hoe. Don't no man want a hoe; he ain't gone never take you home to meet his mama babe. Come to the Lord and let him show you how to be a lady."

"Oh, go to hell old lady," shouted one of the passing girls in the crowd.

"Oh who you talking to hoe? Aunt Lilla ain't got nothing but love for you, but now if you want to go there, Aunt Lilla a take you there. You probably need a good ass whupping anyhow." Aunt Lilla shouted back at the girls in her raspy voice as she began to climb down off of her makeshift podium.

Everybody in Cherry Hill knew that Aunt Lilla carried a gun, and didn't mind shooting it every now and then; so whenever they saw her upset and reaching into her purse, everybody scattered.

The young ladies burst out laughing as they ran down the street from Aunt Lilla-some kicking off their shoes as they ran.

"That's right y'all better run cause um show fixing to beat the hell outta that ass." Aunt Lilla shouted again after the girls, as she slowly turned back around to get back up on her podium. "Going straight to hell anyhow."

"Lilla . . . . Lilla, they just young and out trying to have some fun," said Rose, ushering Aunt Lilla back up on her podium.

"Rose, you know I ain't nothing to play with," said Aunt Lilla. "Um just trying to help them stay outta hell."

She got back up to her podium and stood firmly, and then picked up the Bible and waved it in the air as she spoke to the startled crowd. "See, come to the Lord, and he'll fight all of your battles just like he does mine. See how he had them hoes on the run from an old lady like me."

"Lord have mercy, give me strength." Rose whispered to herself. "Betcha Lilla show keeps her guardian angle so busy."

Rose just bounced around from one person to another, and kept straightening the table with the tracks with her nervous energy. She kept an eye on Aunt Lilla; hoping to keep her out of trouble.

Aunt Lilla watched, through her sermon, as the van carrying Old Joe, Mr. Ire, Miss Eleanor, Big Ma, Aunt Louise, and Uncle Leroy, pull up onto the curve just down from the community center.

"Look Rose," said Aunt Lilla, pointing to the van. "Go take them some tracks fore they get lost in the crowd."

"Huh?"

"Run down there to that van and take them some tracks." Aunt Lilla shouted a little louder.

"Ohhh, ok, ok," said Rose, grabbing a hand full of tracks and running off towards the van.

"And invite them down to hear my sermons." Aunt Lilla shouted after her.

Rose just waved her hand back at Aunt Lilla as she trotted off with the tracks and an abundance of nervous energy running through her veins.

"Come to the Lord while you have a chance, and make heaven your home. You don't have to die and your soul be lost. You been no good all your life, now is the time to straighten up and live right." Aunt Lilla thundered into the microphone. "I use to be low down just like you, but the Lord turned me around; see, and you can be just like me."

Rose heard Aunt Lilla's words vibrating down the street where she was. She hurriedly tossed the tracks into the van, and said a few mumbled words while still looking back at Aunt Lilla. Rose quickly ran off back towards the podium-trying to get back there before Aunt Lilla's words stirred up some more trouble among the passing crowd-for Aunt Lilla spared no one.

"Um just like John the Baptist crying in the wilderness; I'll preach to you the ways of salvation, and even fight you if I have to, to get you to change your hellish ways. I love you just that much." Aunt Lilla said, looking down at the crowd, as they stared interestingly back at her.

Rose, standing at the foot of the make-shift podium, smiled at the passing crowd. She tried silently to mellow the sometimes harsh words that her sister threw out at them.

"Lord help us." Rose whispered to herself. "She means well, and she has a good heart; it's just hard to see sometimes . . . . Of course, Lord you already know that."

CHAPTER THIRTY THREE

"I mean, come on now, how long do we have to sit here waiting on whoever it is that's going to come through that door?" The young purse snatcher shouted towards Snow while crunched down behind an overturned table.

"Just shut up and try to stay alive fool," said Lorna to him without taking her eyes off of the door.

"Well, he does have a point," said V.

"Yea, um with you." Jamaal chimed in.

Snow just ignored them and acted like he didn't hear them. He just continued staring at the front door with his pistols cocked and ready.

Jamaal relaxed, sat back upon the floor and sat his gun down beside him. V stared over at him, and with her pistol still in her hand, and without a word said, she leaped into Jamaal's arms like a lioness upon a young gazelle. She kissed him long a slow. Their lips meshed together as one.

Jamaal wrapped his arms around her and held her tightly. He'd been wanting to do that for weeks, but was trying to be as gentlemanly as possible towards her-trying to show her that he was not just interested in her body.

"Damn, now that's what um talking about." The young purse snatcher said, looking at Lorna and puckering up his lips. "Make love not war; come on, um all yours babe."

"Niggar please, you'd better sit your young ass down somewhere before you get the spanking your young butt so rightly deserve," said Lorna. "That's my man over there." She pointed at Snow.

"For real, that confused white boy over there."

"If I were you, I wouldn't say that too loudly. Just ask anybody who is a dude called Snow." She said.

"All snap, that's Snow," he said, and fell back on his butt. "My bag sister . . . . My bag."

"I've been wanting to do that for weeks, and I dare not let either of us die tonight without at least a kiss." V said as she pulled back and stared into Jamaal's eyes, enjoying his arms being wrapped around her waist.

"Don't worry, we're going to get out of this, no matter what it is; then we'll make our relationship known. God knows these kids need to see a good wholesome loving relationship between a man and a woman."

"Look Romeo and Juliet, why don't we just ease out the back door and get outta here," said the young man sarcastically. "This ain't our fight. Seems to me, whoever it is coming through those doors, got a fight with him-not us." He pointed over at Snow as he spoke.

Jamaal looked at V questioningly as if to say that the young man had a good point.

"No, I cant leave my girl like this; y'all gone. If we come out of this, I'll catch up with you later," said V easing into Jamaal's arms again and holding him tightly as a lone tear ran down her face as she lay her head upon his shoulder; for deep within, though she had made it through some dangerous moment, she felt like she wouldn't make it out of this one, but she just couldn't leave Lorna. Lorna had been there for her too many times. Her heart was torn between her girl and her man; and the thought of losing either of them silently ripped her apart.

"I ain't going nowhere." He said to V, still holding her tightly in his arms, "but, you go, and God willing, we'll catch up with you later." He said to the young man stooping there nervously.

"Go with your man girl. I won't feel hard of you. I choose to die with mine if need be this day." Lorna said, grabbing V's hand. "I waited a long time for a husband, so I ain't fixing to just lose him tonight without fighting with him . . . If Snow dies tonight, then I'll die with him . . . . Go with your man girl."

"You know I can't do that Lorna," V said, now obvious tears rolled down her cheeks.

"No, we can't do that," said Jamaal wiping the tears from V's cheeks.

"We," said the young man. "No, um dipping. Um too young to die; besides, I ain't got no weapon anyway. What um a do, throw chairs at them?"

Lorna kind of rolled her eyes playfully at the young man. "And you wanted to be my man."

"I mean, I ain't no punk, but ain't no need in all of us dieing here tonight. I can go out the back and call the police."

"Who's dieing?" Jamaal snapped.

"No, no police. All of you should leave cause it's not going to be pretty up in here in a little while," said Snow without hardly taking his eyes off of the door. "You too babe; I don't want you to die here tonight; if they didn't kill me, that would. Please Lorna go with them." He now stared over into Lorna's tear filled eyes; his guns still pointing at the door.

Lorna stared back at V, hunched her shoulders, kissed V on the cheek, then ran over to Snow. "You're my man; um with you. We ride or die together." She kissed him on his cheek while rubbing her hand down his long dreads that hang lazily upon his shoulders.

"Now go," said Jamaal to the young man, pointing at the back door.

"Alright, um a try to get some help."

"Remember, be a man in all you do. I am counting on you." Jamaal shouted after him.

The young man swiftly disappeared through the back door.

"I knew he was just a young punk." Lorna said, watching the young purse snatcher quickly run out the back door. "He'll be snatching somebody else's purse by tomorrow."

"Don't be angry babe; this is our fight, not his." Snow whispered, now with a hint of compassion in his voice. "If we make it out of this and end this tonight, we're leaving town and start new some place else and live like normal people."

"Are you serious babe?" Lorna asked like a little child.

"Yea."

"Where we going?" She looked at him with wondering eyes.

"Where ever you like," said Snow, gazing deeply at Lorna, whose eyes were laced with tears.

"Oh hell no, we ain't fixing to die here tonight. We got a wonderful future ahead tomorrow." She repositioned her self and firmly pointed her gun at the front door.

Snow smiled at Lorna's statement. He hadn't prayed in a long time, but tonight he whispered a silent prayer to God, and promised him that if he allowed him to make it out of this tonight, and end this with Mr. Sloan, he would turn his life around, and leave his old path; too, he begged God to please spare Lorna's life tonight-let not another piece of his heart die tonight, as it did with his girl Candy. A wave of sadness showered his heart as he thought of how so hypocritical it was that he was asking God to allow him to kill another man, and himself be spare. Drops of fear tinkled way back in the deep shadow trenches of his mind, for he knew that the God his father served, the God that he had been running from all these years, didn't work like that.

CHAPTER THIRTY FOUR

Dark clouds rolled up in the sky of Cherry Hill; unholy clouds filled with great fiery streaks of lightening that shot forth and lit up the sky every now and then. Thunder silently roared in the distance as though waiting for the clouds to empty themselves upon the somber streets filled with wayward folks still looking to have a good time. Tiny rain drops misted the neon night and splattered upon the begging souls of Cherry Hill.

Off in the distance, beyond the leaning palm trees and rolling hills, brilliant, vibrant colors of sunset lay upon the velvety billowing sky; orange, pink, yellow, and hues of blue meshed together like a newly blossoming flower garden. It was as though, for this one nanno of a second, night and day met and became as one. Heaven and earth fused and erased the boundaries of separation-where you could step out of one, and into the other, where holy and unholy collided and spilled onto the drunken earth beneath. But, the partying folks in Cherry Hill didn't notice the brilliant ominous sky off in the distance.

Young women rushed to get inside to shield their new hairdos from the on coming rain, while others ran to their cars, trying to escape whatever storm was on the way.

Creeping darkness, deep black darkness, filled with unholy moans and muffled screams of suffering and torment eased down the streets and almost swallowed the glimmering lights in Cherry Hill. If you listened hard enough you could almost hear the wind whispering softly of caution to anyone that would listen.

"You in over your head Prince Nathan," said Morrow. "My troops are all here. You can't win this one. Just bow out gracefully. Let that piece of dirt alone"

Nathan didn't utter a word; he just stared, with those piercing penetrating eyes, over at Morrow trying to celebrate even before the battle began. He felt this would be a battle unlike he'd had in a long time; too, he knew that many of his reinforcements were over seas, in some turmoil filled foreign country, fighting Morrow's master-the very powerful Dark Prince of the night; and he could not call for Michael, his prince who reeled much more power than he, for he too was amidst battle. It was as though the cards were stacked for Morrow this night and it would be a battle to remember. He was not backing down, backing down or surrendering was never an option for him; and some how he knew that, this time, Morrow wouldn't either.

Nathan looked at the ever increasing dark sky, riddled with Morrow's reinforcing troops zipping across here and there like bursts of flickering lightening masked by deep darkness.

"I organized this one very well; if I must say so myself." Morrow slowly swept his long skinny fingers through his beard.

"Yea, you're never short on patting your own self on the back. You're so full of yourself and pride; which is what got you in the fix you're in today."

"What fix? I am lord of my kingdom. I go and come as I please."

"You think that you're talking to somebody that doesn't know any better." A fake smile slowly eased across Nathan's face. "Hallelujah, I know who you really are; so drop the act and make believe. You're not talking to a piece of dirt-as you call them."

"See, you didn't have to go there Nathan. I would have had mercy upon the few of you tonight." Morrow whipped with his arched brows and fiery eyes as he looked straight through Nathan.

"Hallelujah always reminds you from whence you came-huh. And, it doesn't take but a few of us to disband an unholy crowd of want to be soldiers."

"Tonight, even you can't believe your own rhetoric, but indeed, I admire your bravery in the midst of pending defeat." He let out a cold feigned laugh.

"All is prepared and ready my prince." A darken figure cloaked in a long black robe with a hood that hid his face hissed to Morrow with his head bowed towards the earth in complete obedience.

Morrow smiled, and again ran his skinny fingers softly through his beard.

"Why hide yourself, for you vainly attempt to hide your identity from me." Nathan pointed to the hooded figure and flicked his finger towards him, and the hood slid quickly from his head. "See, Fear, I already knew that it was you. There be few battles fought without you-though, of course you know that your antics fail among my soldiers."

The shadowed figure just stood there in silence and soaked up the words of Nathan in faked humility. His head lowered, he waited for instructions from Morrow.

"Why risk everything, well, your little pride for a piece of unworthy dirt. There be many others that you can save. Just let this one go. I've invested too much time to let go."

"What is time to us, not even a mist of water amongst the rain drops of eternity. A thousand years is but a moment. How be it, time is something reserve for they that be earth dwellers-confined to walk only upon the dirt." Nathan turned his back, and gazed into the dark sky.

"Now that's what um talking about. You wasting your time on a piece of dirt that abide less than a tree."

"No, I was referring to your rhetoric about investing too much time in Snow."

"Well, um not letting go tonight." He reeled from under his cloak a blazing glimmering blue sword that glistened and threw bursts of blue light upon Nathan's face.

"No you didn't bring the Blue Sword! How'd you get it? Where'd you get it? You can't use that tonight Morrow. Think of what you are doing. You'll slay your brothers over a piece of dirt." Nathan was openly taken aback by the sight of the Blue Sword.

"As I told you, I'll not lose tonight. The question is how much are you willing to lose in a futile attempt to save that dirt the earthlings call Snow." He sliced the air with the Blue Sword as though slicing through an opponent. It sliced the air like silent death seeking a foe to terminate forever.

"You know the story of that sword Morrow. It destroys everything it touches, even its bearer sooner or later. That's why the Creator banished it forever."

The Blue Sword was the only weapon that could annihilate an unearthly being and send them wasted into the realm of nothingness for thousands and thousands of years; all those that it had wounded in the past-even thousands, only a few has yet to return. It was a Sword made, by the Creator himself from bits of heaven and other celestial stores, to eventually, for a time, clean up the celestial shores of those Beings that's so unruly that they attempted to shift even the cosmos out of its holy place.

Morrow was no match for Nathan, even with the Blue Sword, and he knew it, but he also knew that before Prince Nathan could defeat him and take the Blue Sword, he would have banished a great many of his followers, and he knew that Nathan would not take that chance tonight, or so he hoped.

Nathan stood mesmerized gazing hard at Morrow holding the Blue Sword down his side with an ugly grin plastered on his face.

Suddenly a dazzling ball of light eased from the sky and rested adjacent to Nathan; and out of the dazzling light stepped Hope wearing her brilliant smile and big brown eyes gazing at Nathan.

"You shouldn't be here Hope." Nathan grabbed her hand and pulled her close—farther away from Morrow.

"Shall I let my prince battle tonight alone while needing reinforcements?" She gazed up into Nathan's face, and stepped even closer to him. "No, I cannot sit back in the safety of the heavens and watch this unfold. I come to battle along side you my prince."

"Oh, how sweet. Lovers wanting to fall together." Morrow chuckled and leaned hard on the Blue Sword.

"What?" Nathan whipped at him.

"Now, you know that everybody that has a lil sense knows that you and hope have this thing for each other; which um glad, for now I know that during this battle, she is indeed your weakness; your thorn in the flesh. I promise that she shall be amongst the first to taste the bitter nectar of the

Blue Sword, and be banished for thousands of years, if not forever. Can you bare that Prince Nathan?"

Nathan stepped towards Morrow. Hope grabbed him by the arm and pulled him back. "No, that is what he wants you to do," said Hope. "We're not without resource my love; for I knew that someday we would need this."

She reached behind her and pulled out from under her white cloak a dully glimmering golden long dagger with rubies and diamonds imbedded in its handle. The two edged blade curved slightly with unknown writings displayed upon both its sides. The Blue Sword was the Golden Dagger's Nemeses, but unlike the Blue Sword, not only could it kill, but it could also restore life. All the dark soldiers feared the Golden Dagger even much more than the Blue Sword, for even a scratch from the Golden Dagger would send them instantly into oblivion for thousands of years; and, unlike the Blue Sword, the Golden Dagger could not be stolen, or taken away forcefully. It could only be given away by its owner. If ever it was flung at an enemy, it reached its mark and instantly returned to its barer. Too, unlike the Blue Sword, wicked and evil could not harness the Golden Dagger.

Morrow stood speechless, not fully knowing what his next move should be. "Still, Hope shall be amongst my first." He tried to veil his fear and concern.

"Let not that concern you my love, my prince, for I shall gladly go into the abyss for you. I'll leap into it for you; if it shall but save you."

"But you would take my heart with you." Nathan rubbed his palm gently across Hope's face.

"Y'all about to make me gag with all this mushy love stuff."

Before Morrow could barely release his last words, Nathan flicked the Golden Dagger towards him. With the speed of lightening, Morrow easily avoided the lethal dagger, and smiled at Nathan.

"You didn't think I'd be that easy did you?" He whiffed with arrogance.

"No, it wasn't intended for you." Nathan raised his hand, and the Golden Dagger sailed back to him and lodged in his hand with a snap.

Morrow looked around. Fear staggered and dropped to his knees as unholy blood oozed from his chest.

"What! That was stupid." Morrow shouted at Nathan in anger. "You know you cannot banish Fear."

"No, but I can wound him so until he is of little use to you right now."

Fear staggered to his feet, grimaced, peered angrily over his shoulder at Nathan, and then stumbled into the blackness behind Morrow.

There were eight celestial beings that could only be banished by the Creator himself—Fear, Love, Hate, Poverty, Greed,

Faith, Death and life. They roamed where ever they willed around the earth; in every part of the earth-affecting all of the earth dwellers in one way or another. And though Nathan had only seen Fear amidst the dark army, he knew that some of the other eight celestials were there somewhere roaming the ranks, for often times they stood fighting on both sides; but he doubted deeply though, that love would be there.

"I could sure use Faith among our ranks tonight." He gazed deeply into Hope's eyes. "Is she here, or in rout?"

"No my prince; Faith is now bombarded and laboring heavily, as we speak, upon the place the earth walkers call Africa."

"I give you one last chance to reconsider tonight Dark Prince—One last chance only." Nathan yelled amidst a current of anger.

Morrow grunted loudly, and then disappeared into the darkness; but Nathan knew that he would be back soon-real soon—with avenges.

CHAPTER THIRTY FIVE

Mr. Sloan and his men packed into a stolen black van. He slung out last minute instructions and eminent threats. Snows survival was not an option. This must end tonight at any cost. Most of them didn't want to be there, for they felt like the beef was between Snow and Mr. Sloan, but they were too afraid to go against the now insane Mr. Sloan; for thoughts of Snow dominated his every thought every day. He didn't know what corner Snow would be waiting around for him, and he could no longer enjoy his night life in the club because he had to always be on edge-never knowing when Snow might show up and gun him and his men down during their time of celebration and intoxication. Home too, was no refuge; he knew that there was no place beyond Snow's reach. His home was filled with sleepless nights of hearing every little noise, and seeing things in the shadows that wasn't there-no, this had to end tonight; one of them had to die tonight.

The van sped towards Cherry Hill carrying its league of assassins. Every one of them had Snow's name embedded in their trigger fingers and hanging from their muzzles.

"The man that kills Snow will get fifty thousand dollars tonight." Mr. Sloan looked at them with evil eyes and a crooked brow. "No one comes back unless Snow it dead. Y'all got that."

They all nodded their heads, and fumbled with their guns-making sure that they were loaded, cocked, and ready.

Mr. Sloan was obviously nervous; even though he had been drinking to calm his nerves. Secretly, he felt like this night would not end well for him, but he had to go and end it; continuing to live in fear was not an option for him tonight.

"June bug why wouldn't you listen to me? I warned you to stay away from Snow, and have no dealings with him. I told you he was not a man that you wanted to cross." He argued silently at his fallen son that Snow had killed. "All this would not be happening if you had just listened; now, tonight, I might very well be joining you, for I didn't take my own advice I gave to you . . . . Damn you June bug." He slammed his fist onto the dashboard.

"What if Snow is not at the Community Center?" One of the assassins muttered.

"Oh he'll be there. I planted a snitch to tell him that we were coming."

"You mean to tell me that he knows we're coming, so he's there waiting for us." One of the men snapped.

"Yea, but he knows not when we shall come. He's probably thinking that we'll come late tonight, but we'll start the party early."

Now the men were convinced that Mr. Sloan was out of his mind; they were probably the ones walking into a trap.

"This might be a trap then."

"You questioning me?" Mr. Sloan rubbed the barrel of his gun across his face as he spoke.

"No, um just saying." He slid hard back in his seat and held on tightly to his gun.

"Don't worry, we going to get him, and one of you is going to be fifty thousand dollars richer." Mr. Sloan no longer believed his own rhetoric. Fear rested heavily upon his shoulders.

Disdain eased across all of their faces, as they swayed slowly back and forth to the rhythm of the moving van, for they now realize that it was they that were walking into a trap amidst an unholy war led by a man whose guide was insanity.

CHAPTER THIRTY SIX

"Lilla, can we go home early tonight?" Humbly, Rose stared up the podium at Aunt Lilla. "Um tired and I don't feel well."

"Now Rose you know I don't quit this early in the night. Did Jesus quit on us?"

"No, but he ain't have to be on his feet all day and then come and try to watch over a crazy woman all night." Rose whispered to herself as she slid her shoe off and reached down and massaged her foot.

"Huh?"

"Nothing Lilla."

"You said something. You ain't crazy is you? Down there talking to yourself."

"No, I ain't crazy. You got enough of that for both of us." Rose whispered again to herself.

"What? I can't hear you."

"Nothing Lilla, nothing; um just talking to myself."

"If the Lord comes back tonight, will you be ready?" Aunt Lilla belted out at the young man passing by.

The young man ignored her and just kept walking steadily along; no doubt, abiding in his own young world with his own host of young problems. The most prominent thing about problems and troubles is that they don't discriminate on whom they shall come; they abide upon the young, the old, the rich, the poor, the healthy, and the sick-all in this life will have their complete share of problems and troubles. This young man was not scared, for his facial expression unveiled hints of his toils-he just kept walking, trying to ignore the old lady irritating him hollering from the table top across the street.

"And pull your pants up on your butt; nobody wants to see all that. A real man will at least keep his pants up."

He had tried to hurry along and ignore her, but she was too persistent; and he would have been successful in ignoring her if the young girls standing on the adjacent corner were not staring at him and listening to Aunt Lilla's remarks while they giggled amongst themselves.

He raised his hand high into the air, and shot his middle finger at Aunt Lilla.

The young girls on the adjacent corner giggled even louder at his provocative gesture to Aunt Lilla.

"Oh hell no your young butt didn't." Aunt Lilla tossed the microphone aside and jumped down off the table. "Um fixing to whup that ass."

Rose scrambled to get in front of Aunt Lilla. "Will you leave that young boy alone Lilla; just let him go upon his way."

"He don't know me like that Rose; I'll spank his young butt tonight like his mama should have done a long time ago."

"Just let him go Lilla. The other folks need to hear your words; now get back up there and let that boy go about his way." Rose had her arms wrapped around Aunt Lilla's shoulders while trying to reason with her, pressing her lips hard upon Aunt Lilla's ear as she spoke.

"Ok . . . . Ok . . . . Um going back up and keep preaching, but his young ass better keep stepping."

Though he had slowed down, for he didn't want to appear to be running from the old lady in front of the girls, he kept moving towards his destination.

Aunt Lilla resumed her preaching. "You can be ready when the Lord comes back. All you have to do is accept the Lord Jesus Christ as your savior, and you'll be ready. If you don't let him into your hearts, you'll spend eternity in hell."

The young girls across the street still looked, whispered, pointed, and giggled hard at Aunt Lilla.

"Lord let them young gals move on." Rose waved her hand to the young girls, trying to get them to move on; she knew that they were brewing trouble.

They just giggled even more.

"You don't want to go to hell! Come and I'll help you out of hell." Aunt Lilla looked sternly at the young girls as she preached; now a bit irritated at them.

She slowly closed her bible, and peered hard over at the young girls as she pondered deeply. "What y'all thank y'all looking at—TV. I ain't no comical show. This is serious business."

The girls just wouldn't stop giggling at Aunt Lilla.

"That's the very reason why y'all young hoes going to hell right now, but before you go to hell, Aunt Lilla's going to whup that ass."

She started climbing down off the table. Rose, now franticly waved at the girls to move on. Aunt Lilla straightened her dress, and then started to trot towards the young girls-Rose right on her heals pulling at her dress.

"Turn me lose Rose."

The young girls started to run away amidst laughter.

"That's right, your young butts better run!" She hollered after them waving her fists in the air. "Rose will you turn me lose. Sometimes I worry bout you Rose."

Rose held onto Aunt Lilla's dress so tight until it hurt her hand; she could hardly unclench her fist.

Aunt Lilla climbed back up on her makeshift podium, and looked back at Rose and shook her head. Her love for Rose was only equaled by Rose love for her. The only family that they had was each other. Aunt Lilla was a little too coarse for organized traditional religion. They didn't know how to take her; so she started preaching on the streets. Rose came along to keep her out of trouble-knowing full well how quickly Aunt Lilla's temper could flare up.

CHAPTER THIRTY SEVEN

"That's the funniest religious woman I've ever seen; just throwing the tracks at us. Boy, wasn't she in a hurry." Mr. Ire mumbled loudly to Old Joe as he watched Rose hurry off back to the yelling woman on the corner.

"Yea, Jesus must be in a hurry tonight." Uncle Leroy giggled to himself along with Old Joe and Mr. Ire.

"See, that's the very reason why you going to bust hell wide open." Big Ma grabbed her purse and slung it across her shoulders.

"Let's just gone in and see Frank Junior," said Old Joe with a big smile.

"Yes Joseph, let's do that." Miss Eleanor grabbed Old Joe's hand and pulled him forth towards the Community Center.

They all walked casually towards the double doors at the Center. Miss Eleanor was nervous; for she hadn't seen Frank Junior since the bombing-when she had lost Julia and her family, and T.C and Poochie. She pondered what to say to Frank Junior when she first saw him-she must convince him to leave this life style; she thought to herself.

They opened the double doors, and walked through into a haze of loud music blasting from the radio while Snow and the others inside lay crouched behind overturned tables and chairs.

"What the hell." Uncle Leroy exclaimed, looking hard and surprised at Snow and the others hiding behind the tables. "Is there something y'all need to tell us?"

"That's what um talking bout." Big Ma chimed in.

Just as Snow started to lift from behind the corner, A loud thunder echoed through the room as a bullet exploded through the double doors and tore through Big Ma's back and put a gaping hole in her chest-her aorta severed completely from her heart, she was dead instantly-before her body could even hit the floor. With her last reflexes, she grabbed Uncle Leroy and Aunt Louise in her arms as her body towered towards the floor, trying, with her last breath, to protect her children; though she and Uncle Leroy argued most of the time, she loved him as a son, and just as much as she loved her daughter Aunt Louise.

"Oh God, Mama . . . . Mama!" Aunt Louise screamed with blood splattered across her face.

"Madear . . . Madear . . . ." Uncle Leroy shouted the terms of endearment that he only called Big Ma when he was in trouble.

Old Joe grabbed Miss Eleanor and started to pull her to the ground, but before he could, a maze of bullets barreled through the double doors and found Old Joe's and Miss Eleanor's warm inviting flesh. They ripped through their bodies like a hot knife through warm butter. Old Joe and Miss Eleanor's blooded bodies slammed to the floor while another multitude of burning bullets followed Mr. Ire as he leaped behind some tables adjacent to the double doors.

Aunt Louise kept screaming in panic as the last drops of warm blood oozed from Big Ma's chest and rested upon her shoulders. Uncle Leroy scrambled to get from under Big Ma's arm.

"No . . . . No . . . . Stay down . . . . Stay down; Snow screamed at them."

But, it was no use, Uncle Leroy was frantic and kept trying until he freed himself. He lifted up to go to Aunt Louise. On his knees he started to reach over to Aunt Louise, but before his hand could touch her outstretched hand, a storm of melting bullets screamed when they smashed through the riddled double doors. As their hands touch, the two of them fell limp across Big Ma's body-their blood mingled with Big Ma's already clotting rich red blood.

Mr. Ire slid hard under some chairs, and quickly crawled behind a desk.

"Ire, you hit?" Snow hollered above the roaring screaming bullets.

"No, um alright I think."

"Here." Snow slid one of his guns down the bar like stand to Mr. Ire.

"Yea, bring it on you good for nothing roaches." Mr. Ire looked over at Old Joe, Miss Eleanor, Big Ma, Aunt Louise, and Uncle Leroy lying on the floor showered in blood, but he was too hyped up to fill anything but anger. He was in war mode; it was now time to kill or be killed. He would have the luxury to be sad, hurt, and sympathetic later on-now, was a time to stay alive, or join them that were dead, or dieing.

"Why we ain't shooting back?" Jamaal yelled at V above the thunder.

"What we gone shoot at. We need to see our targets."

"If we shoot back, they'll know that we got guns too."

"Oh they know that we have guns."

"How? I haven't seen the shooters."

"Cause they know he's in here." V pointed over at Snow.

Suddenly, masked men in black suits came running through the torn double doors shooting as they came. Snow and the others welcomed them with hot bullets and smoking barrels.

"Die you damned cock roaches! Die!" Mr. Ire hollered while pulling his trigger and sending hot bullets flying searching for a target.

CHAPTER THIRTY EIGHT

Winds gusted and whistled down the streets and allies of Cherry Hill, as orange clouds with hues of red mixed violently with pushing dark black clouds filled with thunder and lightening.

Those that had not left Cherry Hill could not leave now of their on. The war in the heavens, and on the earth had started, and neither wanted to take prisoners or surrender, or retreat. Tonight was the ending-one way or the other; this war would end tonight.

The natural and the supernatural, angels and demons, the holy and unholy, all fought tonight on the same battle field, seeking reckoning for bygone sins of either side.

With the speed of light, Morrow lunched at Nathan with the Blue Sword . . . . swish . . . . swish . . . . swish, was all you could hear as the Blue Sword sliced through the air, missing Prince Nathan by a mile.

"You are no match for me Morrow; why be banished for naught." Nathan said smoothly while easily avoiding the piercing edge of the Blue Sword.

Hope screamed loudly as she fought off a band of darkened unholy dissidents. Even by herself, usually, Hope was a force to be reckoned with for these lost evil ones, but tonight, there was just too many of them; too many attacking her at the same time.

Finally, with all of her strength almost depleted, she yielded to them. They pounced upon her like torrents of winds of a hurricane when it first reach dry land.

"See, Prince Nathan, I was really merely diverting your attention so that my soldiers could surrender Hope without interference from you."

Hope now unconscious, slumped as they dragged her off towards a mass of darken angry clouds.

Nathan heard Hope's screams of anger, and from the corner of his eyes, he could see that she had fallen limp, and was about to be carried away into evil oblivion by Morrow's evil lieutenants.

As a burst of light, he slung the golden dagger at Morrow while at the very same time flying, even faster than light itself, to Hopes rescue; and with more than the strength of a nuclear weapon, he freed hope from the hands of her defiled captors.

Morrow held Hope in one arm, and held his free hand high into the air. The Golden Dagger snapped loudly as it landed back into the palm of his hand.

"Damn you prince!" Morrow screamed out amidst anger, signaling for his dark army to attack.

The unholy war in the heavens were now fully lunched while the war between the earthen vessels beneath spilled on.

Black drops of rain sprinkled upon the violent streets of Cherry Hill; black rain drops that were the pain filled tears of the evil dark ones falling in battle.

CHAPTER THIRTY NINE

Rose slid up under the table, trying to shield herself from the black raindrops falling from the blacken sky, and the thunder of bullets screaming down the street.

"What the hell is this?" Aunt Lilla exclaimed, quickly jumping down off the table. "Lord ham mercy."

"Lilla you'd better get out of that black stuff."

Aunt Lilla looked down the street at the men in dark suits spitting a barrage of bullets into the Community Center.

"Lilla, get down . . . . Get down." Rose screamed out, trying to grab the hem of Aunt Lilla's dress.

Black raindrops streaked down Aunt Lilla's brow and rested under her chin. She stared hard at the commotion at the Community Center as anger built up and overflowed in her bosom. Nobody is going to help them. Everybody outside of the Community Center is running trying to hide and protect themselves-she thought to herself.

"See, that's what's wrong with us; we always too scared to do anything. Let these niggars from outside come in Cherry Hill and tare up what we trying to build up; but not this time . . . . Not on my watch." She reached back and grabbed her purse, fumbled through it, and found her 38 pistol.

"Lilla you come back here . . . . Lilla . . . . Lilla." Rose screamed after Aunt Lilla. "Darn!"

Rose climbed out from under the table, trying hard to avoid the black raindrops. She was scared and terrified; not knowing what the black raindrops were, or when a stray bullet might tare through her big sister. She ran after Aunt Lilla, Aunt Lilla walked briskly, resolute on helping the victims inside the Community Center. She lifted her gun, aimed, and fired a bullet down at the attackers in the black suits. It hit one of the assassins and rested in his shoulder as he yelled out in pain.

Rose ran in front of Aunt Lilla and threw her arms around her. "Lilla . . . . Lilla . . . . You gone get both of us killed."

"Get out of the way Rose. Somebody got to stand up and help them . . . . Get out my way."

Suddenly Rose fell limp into Aunt Lilla's arms. A bullet had hit her at the base of her neck. Aunt Lilla screamed at the top of her lungs.

"Rose . . . . Rose . . . . Rose!!" She screamed, filling Rose warm blood ease upon her large hands.

Rose just lay there in her arms; her hazel eyes staring blankly into the angry sky as black raindrops leaped from her face and smashed to the already wet sidewalk.

"Rose! Rose!" She tried desperately not to let Rose fall hard onto the pavement. She could feel the vibration of other bullets piercing Rose back-shielding her. "You don't have to protect me no more Rose . . . . Rose!"

She fell to the sidewalk holding the weight of Rose. Her sister now gone; taken by some unknown killers-killers that wasn't even from Cherry Hill. The only family she had; the only one that truly understood her, put up with her, was now taken away. Her life was done. She knew it. She laid Rose aside, kissed her on the cheek, and rose to her feet-gun still in hand.

Aunt Lilla, with Rose's blood dripping from her hand, and black raindrops pelting her face, limped hard towards the assassins, still attacking the Community Center. She pointed and squeezed her trigger until all of her bullets were spent, and having run out of bullets, she limped on while throwing the empty 38 at the assassins.

A storm of hot bullets ripped through Aunt Lilla's torso. She hit the ground hard and rolled to a stop-half her body on the sidewalk and half on the road. The last bits of Aunt Lilla's life leaked out onto the road, and black raindrops carried her blood and emptied it into the sewer drains along the road.

CHAPTER FORTY

"See, I knew we shouldn't have come over here. I knew it! But, would you listen . . . . Noooo . . . . Nooooo . . . . Nooooo . . . . You just had to come to Cherry Hill tonight." Willie thundered at Quitta above the noise of raging gun fire.

Quitta crunched down as far as she could behind some overturned garbage cans. "Will you shut the hell up and do something."

"What? What um a do? Throw some trash at them. Boy, that would certainly stop them-huh. I'll trash them to death!"

"Oh stop being a whiny punk and get us out of here." She snapped at Willie. "Lord if you'll just get us out of this mess, I promise um going to church every Sunday from now on . . . . And, oh yea, I won't have sex with Willie no more until we get married." She whispered a prayer, and hoped that God was listening, though she felt that they were not on good speaking terms.

"Ok, wait here; I'll be right back with the car." Willie dashed from behind the trash cans and darted for his car.

"Willie! Willie! What the hell you doing?"

A bullet hit Willie's right leg. He slammed to the pavement yelling in pain. Quitta ducked out, grabbed Willie by the arm, and pulled him back behind the garbage cans.

"Oh god! Oh god! I feel my whole life running out of me. Um passing fast Quitta."

"Hold on baby . . . . Hold on."

Quitta tore Willie's pants to get a good look at the bullet wound.

"Oh god! Take care yourself Q. Um almost gone. The pain is too intense, but um a man. I'll take it to the end . . . . Oh god Q."

Quitta threw Willie's wounded leg to the side, and stared hard at him with a smirk look on her face.

"What? What?"

"You just got a scratch; luckily."

"Well, how was I to know. Felt like my leg was tore off."

Willie crawled deeper behind the overturned garbage cans and held Quitta close; deciding to wait it out. They would run out of bullets sooner or later. Quitta tucked her head into Willie's chest; smelling the musk of his masculine body somehow made her feel safe.

CHAPTER FORTY ONE

The assassins kept leaping through the doors of the Community Center, some stumbling over the dead bodies of Big Ma, Aunt Louise, Uncle Leroy, Miss Eleanor, and Old Joe as they came. They were falling like flies, and like flies, they just kept coming.

Mr. Ire ran out of bullets; he reached over and grabbed a bottle of gin from the floor, for many bottles had fallen onto the floor during the commotion. Lorna had gotten several boxes of alcohol for a party to celebrate their opening the next day.

He threw that bottle with all of his might. It smashed one assassin smack in the head. He crashed hard to the floor.

Mr. Ire reached over and grabbed another bottle, and started to throw, then looked at what he was about to throw. "Ooh . . . . Ooh, can't throw you. Can't waist good Tequila on cock roaches." It was a big bottle of Patron silver.

"Um out of bullets!" V screamed over at Lorna.

"Me too!" Jamaal shouted loudly, and leaned over and grabbed a piece of board for a weapon.

"Here!" Lorna slid her hot pistol towards V. It stopped a few feet out of her reach. She grabbed the M16, and pointed it at the assassins at the front door.

Only two assassins left standing, shooting; still no signs of Mr. Sloan. Snow aimed, took a deep breath, and then squeezed two bullets sailing to the assassins. Silence eased upon the Community Center like a wondering ghost. The barrel of Snow's pistol was hot with disappearing vapors of spent bullets smoke rose to the ceiling.

"Is it over?" V shouted over at Lorna.

Lorna looked at Snow; she knew to follow whatever Snow did. He crouched there gazing at the front door. With his thumb, he clicked the magazine release button on the side of his pearl handled pistol, and the almost empty magazine fell to the floor. Snow clicked a full magazine back into the chamber in an instant without ever even taken his eyes off of the shattered double doors.

"Reach in my belt and throw Mr. Ire a clip." Snow whispered softly.

"Who's Mr. Ire?"

"The old man over there behind the tables."

"Mr. Ire!" Lorna yelled to the old man peeping from behind the tables.

"Yea!"

She threw the clip over to him. Hurriedly, Mr. Ire snapped the clip into the gun, pulled the chamber back, and then pointed at the front doors.

"I said is it over?" V looked hard at Lorna and Snow.

"No, just stay where you are."

"Cover me; um fixing to get that clip of bullets my girl slid to me."

"With what? Um out of bullets too."

"Just throw the board at him or something if another of them come threw those doors." She leaped out and grabbed the clip and started to retreat back to her hiding place; just then, a bullet thundered and smashed into her side-delivering mounds of pain. V screamed and fell to the floor.

Lorna started to go to her, but Snow pulled her back.

Mr. Sloan leaped threw the double doors, blasting as he came-spitting bullets everywhere with a machine gun. Suddenly his gun jammed; he threw it to the floor and leaped back threw the riddled double doors. Mr. Ire emptied his click at Mr. Sloan as he leaped, but none found its mark.

Snow jumped from his cover, gun still pointing at the front doors, and ran after Mr. Sloan.

Lorna ran over to V. "Um a call an ambulance."

"In Cherry Hill? Please!" Jamaal whipped while pressing a towel to V's side. "Let's put her in my car and take her. It's right outside."

Mr. Sloan, running hard, fumbled with his clip trying desperately to reload while running. He leaped around a corner; bullets barely missing him.

Snow following hard behind, shooting as he went, kept his eyes only on Mr. Sloan-hoping a bullet would hit him at any moment.

CHAPTER FORTY TWO

Demons and angels filled the sky, fighting over the outcome on earth—over the one soul that Morrow needed to destroy; the soul that he had spent much time influencing for an untimely demise-Snow. He didn't rightly know what the Creator had for Snow, but he could see the mark upon his forehead-the mark that was invisible to human eyes. It was the mark that shouted that Snow was anointed for something.

Morrow had no power to destroy Snow, or change his anointing, but he could influence Snow to walk contrary, thereby hindering the anointing on him.

Hues of orange filled the heavens, and eased slowly to the earth like wondering smoke. It was the mingled blood of wounded angels and demons. The battle between the Holies and the unholy raged on.

Nathan, fighting hard, still held Hope in one arm. Suddenly, he felt the penetrating pain in his back from the Blue Sword. Desperately, he tried, with all of his might, to fight on and shield his beloved Hope, but it was no use; the demons attack was too vicious, and unrelenting. Another burst of pain; the Blue Sword pierced him again. Nathan could fight no longer. He held Hope as tightly as he could while the last bit of consciousness eased from him. Like a falling star, he plundered towards the earth at blinding speed as angelic blood oozed from his fatal wounds. He and Hope slammed to the earth like a angry meteor thrown from the dark sky. The Golden Dagger rolled from his hand and dully glistened in the night. No one dared even touch it, for all knew the power of the Golden dagger.

Morrow stood over them with a smirk smile upon his face. "You should have listened to me dear prince. This could have been avoided." He chuckled as he flew off to try to finish off Snow with his evil unholy influence.

Nathan and Hope's bodies, he still holding her tightly in his arms, began to glow hues of neon blue as their Holy bodies began to feel the transition into a thousand years of oblivion.

CHAPTER FORTY THREE

Cautiously, Snow, with his gun pointing out front, darted around the corner. A burst of pain blasted his chest as a bullet tore threw him and knocked him several feet back.

"Damn, finally got your ass!" Mr. Sloan shouted, now walking towards Snow. He pulled his trigger again, but only a loud click filled the air.

Snow, lying upon his back stretched out as though on a cross, gun still in hand pointing towards approaching Sloan, lifted his gun, and aimed-blood now oozing from the corner of his mouth.

Mr. Sloan stopped in his tracks looking down the barrel of Snow's pistol. "Now hold on dog; both of us don't have to die tonight. You lost; accept it." He pleaded.

Snow, still aiming, listened as Mr. Sloan pleaded. He started to squeeze the trigger. Suddenly a thousand memories raced through his head-memories of his family, of happy days when he was just a boy; memories of his father preaching, and his mother sitting in the congregation shouting words of encouragement to her husband; memories of him and Julia playing together, and Julia trying to keep him out of trouble. A smile slowly rested upon Snow's face as the blood still oozed from the corner of his mouth.

He eased off of the trigger, still staring at Mr. Sloan as showers of forgiveness enveloped him. Loads of years of hate and anger eased from him like the last smoke of a smothering fire. He felt rivers of peace; peace he had never felt before, showered down upon him. Slowly, he lowered his gun to the ground while the last drops of life began to leave him. He closed his eyes and prayed to himself, asking God to forgive him for all the retched things that he had done, and to please protect Lorna and Mr. Ire.

"Yes . . . Yes . . . I won! Now, June Bug can rest in peace." Mr. Sloan Celebrated as he turned a corner.

"Sloan." A man shouted, stepping out from the unholy shadows.

Mr. Sloan stopped; it was one of his assassins. He smiled. "You made it too-huh."

"Yea, but you didn't." He sent a bullet slamming into Mr. Sloan's chest. "All of us agreed that you wasn't coming back either-whether Snow lived or died. We couldn't trust you any more old man." He sent several more bullets into Mr. Sloan, and then disappeared into the night.

Mr. Sloan lay upon the cool sidewalk dead; his body completely swallowed by the darken night except for one of his legs lay in the light twitching for a moment-then slowly stopped. After winning his last battle, Mr. Sloan violently entered into eternity like all mortal men will do someday. Darken shadows engulfed him, and like lazy dust during a wind storm, he was whiffed away never to be seen again.

Still wearing that smile, Snow's eyes rolled back into his head. He gave up the last of his life still whispering a prayer for his wife and his friend.

Morrow, bathing in what seemed to be victory, smiled broadly as he stood upon a roof top and looked down upon Snow, then over at disappearing Nathan and Hope as they lay dead still in each other's arms.

The war in the heavens had ceased, and the war on the earth, in this little section of Cherry Hill, too, had come to a stop.

"This is sooooo sweet . . . . Next! Wonder what my next project shall be."

As Morrow spoke, suddenly, hurricane winds swept through the city, as bolts of lightening lit up the sky-chasing away all the darkened shadows.

Suddenly, an unseen force hit the ground with unyielding masses of energy. It made the ground move like waves of the sea, ripping apart the pavement and buildings in Cherry Hill like paper. A mass of brilliant light, a million times brighter than the sun itself, rested in the cradle of earth that it had made.

"No . . . . No . . . . No . . . . This can't be . . . . It's not fare . . . . It's just not fare. I won . . . . I won!!" Morrow scream towards the brilliant light.

"The Creator does what He wants. Have you forgotten Black Prince Morrow? Have you forgotten that He is all supreme?" A magnified voice echoed towards Morrow.

Morrow recognized that voice, for he had previously been trained and subject to its owner for thousands of years. "Gable! Why the Creator would interfere for this peace of dirt? It's not like he's one of us. He's just a piece of fashioned dirt."

"Dirt that the Creator purposed."

"Why have rules if we're not going to follow them?"

"If I were you, I'd taste my words very carefully before I utter them. That which the Creator fashioned is more than a bunch of rules. It is a piece of him," said Gable standing there so tall amidst the brilliant light of the Creator. "Now bow down before you are banished forever."

Morrow, like an obedient kitten bowed himself to the earth in fear, shaking and trembling.

The Creator's all consuming glowing light moved slowly to where Nathan and Hope had fallen. The earth beneath him crumbled with his every step, though his feet never completely touched the ground. A glowing hand, bigger than the body of a large grown man, reached out from the light, and waved over the cradle of Nathan and Hope; and instantly, like rekindling vapors of smoke, and gathering swirling particles of dust, Nathan and Hope's bodies reassembled and appeared without their wounds.

Instantly, they lay prostrate upon their faces, reverencing the Creator, and thanking Him for bringing them back from oblivion.

The Creator moved briskly to Snow lying on the cool pavement now dead with his gun still in his hand. The light shined brightly upon Snow's blooded body. The Creator waved his had across Snow's still body. Snow's eyes flickered, and he coughed and sat up. With a radiant smile on his face, he looked into the Creator's light. The Creator's glowing hand came forth from the light and touched Snow upon the forehead, and he fell back as though asleep. A mark glowed upon Snow's head like a glimmering star.

Slowly the Creator began to ascend back to the sky; the earth beneath him, which had crumbled at his every step, began to reassemble itself as though it had never been disturbed. Buildings began to come back together in their original state. The Creator kelp ascending higher and higher into the night sky-glowing like the sun as he went; then suddenly, He disappeared as though He had never been.

Sirens echoed in the background from the distant approaching police cars.

Gable lifted his hand, and the sirens went silent. "One more earthly moment before we exit. Morrow, help Snow and his friends exit this place before the mortal law keepers come."

"What? Me help that dirt . . . . why that's insult to injury."

"It be but little punishment for what you have done; I could banish you forever, but the Creator is merciful."

Gable pointed to an old SUV truck that had suddenly appeared beside the road with its engine running; Morrow began walking towards the truck, while doing so, his image changed, and he became a black man in jeans and a pullover shirt.

Morrow looked down at his self as he trotted forth. "For real Gable . . . I mean, for real . . . . come onnnn. I look like a piece of dirt."

Gable just looked at Morrow and smirked while Nathan and Hope snickered and looked on.

"The faster you get them out of here, the quicker you return to your self." Gable shouted at Morrow.

Morrow jumped in the truck and squealed his tires over to unconscious Snow. He got out and pulled Snow into the truck, and then sped off to the Community Center.

Lorna and Jamaal held V around her waist as they all came limping out of the Community Center. Mr. Ire now allowed himself to grieve over his fallen friends while he thanked God for allowing him to survive this brutal assault. He wondered had Snow made it; he hoped and prayed.

The tires, on the SUV that Morrow and Snow was in, screamed as it came to a stop in front of Lorna and the others.

"Get in," said Morrow as he jumped out of the truck to assist them.

"Who are you?" Mr. Ire asked cautiously.

"Who cares, we got to get my girl to the hospital."

Once again sirens filled the air from approaching police cars.

"Come onnnnn, get in. Does it really matter who I am . . . . I mean, for real. Does it really matter right now?" Morrow ushered them into the truck. V moaned loudly from pain, and then slumped unconscious.

Lorna ran around to the front passenger side of the truck where Snow lay unconscious. She jumped in and squeezed herself next to him. "Oh baby! Is he alright?" She kissed him upon his forehead, and tried to examine his wounds.

"Wait, he ain't got no wounds, so where did all this blood come from."

"Other folks blood." Morrow grumbled as he rolled his eyes in disgust.

"Old man Sloan?" V asked.

"Yea right . . . . whatever."

They sped off, passing speeding police cars as they went.

"Hurry man, go to John F. Kennedy Hospital fast!!" Jamaal shouted. "You hold on babe, um not about to lose you now."

"Um hurrying! Just so fast you can go in this mortal means of transport."

"Huh?"

"Er, um just saying, we'll be there in a minute. She'll not be banished."

"What?"

"She's going to survive is all um saying."

They looked at each other and hutched their shoulders in confusion about this man called Morrow that they just met; they thought that he was weird, and Mr. Ire thought to himself that he'd better keep an eye on him.

Snow's eyes trickled opened. He looked into Lorna's eyes and smiled broadly.

"You scared us for a minute. Are you alright?" Lorna rubbed her hands through Snow's dreadlocked hair.

"Yea, um cool. It's finally over."

"You for real babe?"

"Yea." Snow replied weakly.

They roared up to the front of the emergency room. "Now get out!"

"Huh."

"I mean, we're here. Go inside and let them patch y'all up."

Snow leaned forward, and looked over at Morrow. "You?"

"Yea, it's me, but not for long."

"But you're . . . ." Snow fell back in his seat-weak.

"Just get out . . . . No, I tell you what; y'all just keep the truck. I've got to go." Morrow ran off into the shadows across the street.

"He is one weird dude," said Jamaal.

The nurses brought a stretcher out and carried V off to surgery. Lorna drove the truck into the parking lot, and she and Snow talked for a good long time of their future. Snow was somehow different; she could tell.

"God spared me; I know what I am supposed to do now. We're going to leave this place and start over as soon as V is ok. I know what my Calling is!!"

"Your Calling?"

"I'll explain it to you later. Let's go check on the others." Snow eased out of the truck with a little help from Lorna.

Morrow watched them from the shadows. "Pathetic piece of dirt." He looked down at himself; he was still clothed in an earthen body. "Come onnnn Gable, I've finished what you asked me to do."

"Do you good to be a piece of dirt for awhile." A voice rang out from the heavens. "Now go join yourself with them until you are summoned back."

"What . . . . What . . . . But I did what I was told."

"Want to be banished?"

"Ok . . . Ok . . . . Ok . . . Um going . . . . Um going."

Morrow went back into the emergency room and waited for V with the rest of them-pouting about being bound to his new earthen body.

Snow sat there huddled next to Lorna while she tried to clean him up with a wet paper towel. He sat smiling and staring off into space. "I know what I am supposed to do now." He kept saying.

"I think you ought to let them check Snow out too. He probably took a hard hit to the head." Mr. Ire whispered into Lorna's ear.

"He'll be alright; he's just a little confused right now."

"No, I am not confused; I've never been more sure of things, and never felt better. I am at peace with myself, my fellow man, and God. Snow died back there, I am a new man . . . . Frank; that's what my grandmother had been praying for. Now I know that my redeemer lives . . . . God is real!!!"

CHAPTER FORTY FOUR

Nathan and hope firmly held hands as they gazed up at the sky and watched the dark clouds roll away with the fallen angels easing off to other places to foil. They turned and looked deeply into each other's eyes-knowing full well that they had to be off to their duties.

"I know . . . I know . . . . You've got to go," said Nathan. "The world would be a mighty sad place without you, but I shall miss you Hope-my heart is forever with you. This night has only mended our hearts closer."

"I know my prince . . . . I know. Maybe someday we'll be able to spend some real time together-when my dear sister Peace will have conquered the world; but now, I must be off to some place in the East call Iran to assist my other sister Love."

Nathan raised his hand high into the air, and the Golden dagger snapped back into the palm of his hand, and then they both vanished in an instant journeying to their places of duty.